KT-458-467

The Range Shootout

James Buckley Armstrong, or Buck to his friends, has been asked to look after a company of palaeontologists as they search for dinosaur bones on rangeland owned by Big John Calhoun. Stumbling onto a bunch of rustlers is only the first problem he faces.

Called a rustler and a liar by Big John's stepson, Buck is saved by the rancher's older son, Cord, after being kidnapped and left to die. Then a stagecoach hold-up is blamed on Buck and Cord and the manhunt is on.

Only when mysteries are solved and questions answered can Buck win through.

By the same author

Buck and the Widow Rancher

The Range Shootout

Carlton Youngblood

A Black Horse Western

ROBERT HALE · LONDON

© William Sheehy 2007
First published in Great Britain 2007

ISBN 978-0-7090-8216-3

Robert Hale Limited
Clerkenwell House
Clerkenwell Green
London EC1R 0HT

The right of William Sheehy to be identified as
author of this work has been asserted by him
in accordance with the Copyright, Designs and
Patents Act 1988

BOLTON LIBRARIES	
12054003	
Bertrams	25.02.07
	£11.25

Typeset by
Derek Doyle & Associates, Shaw Heath
Printed and bound in Great Britain by
Antony Rowe Limited, Wiltshire

CHAPTER 1

The tall rider on the big black stud horse sat comfortably in the saddle, listening to the late morning silence and enjoying his view of the emptiness ahead. Smiling at the peacefulness of it all, he took the tobacco sack from a shirt-pocket and quickly rolled his cigarette as he looked out over the flat land. He twisted the ends, struck a wooden match on a denim-clad pants leg, and put flame to the quirly.

When he'd finished his smoke he pinched out the fire, touched a heel to his horse and continued on his way at a ground-eating trot. As he came around one of the larger juniper thickets he pulled sharply back on the reins, stopping the horse at the very edge of a ravine. Actually it was too wide to be a real coulée or ravine and while he could see the other side, the grassland below spread out of sight in both directions. Not a coulée but more like a canyon or a shallow basin, it was only ten or twenty feet to the bottom. Buck was amazed to see grass: thick, knee-deep wild-oat grass from the look of it, that covered the bottom land from one side to the other, broken by a thick line of willows meandering from one end to the other.

Right there, in the middle of nowhere, was a cattleman's dream. From where he sat, he couldn't see just how long the basin was. But what he could see had to cover fifty or sixty acres, he judged.

Sitting in the shade of the junipers, he watched as a small herd of deer moved silently out of the willows and, feeding between long searching looks, slowly moved along the bottom. The black's head jerked up in the same instant that the deer vanished into the safety of the creek bottom. Almost at the same time he heard it, the thundering of horses running. Buck pulled back a little into the deeper late-morning shade of the junipers and watched as a half-dozen or so horses came pouring down the near side of the basin. Hard on their tails was a handful of riders, pushing the horses with yells and the whip-ends of their lariats. As quickly as they appeared and rushed by, they were gone. Almost as quickly the sound of their passing faded. Buck figured the basin turned, taking the herd and the riders out of range.

So, he thought sadly, he wasn't as alone in the world as he had hoped. Well, maybe that wasn't so bad. If there were riders, there must be either a ranch or at least a chuck wagon. As it was nearing suppertime, maybe the welcome mat would be out. After all, it was a custom that no rider got turned away from a meal, especially at mealtime.

Smiling again, the rider gigged the big horse down the soft dirt bank and out into the grassy bottomland and followed the swath laid down by the running horses. This, as any livestock man would tell you, was near perfect grazing-land; grass that would dry into good winter feed even during the often severe cold snaps that hit this part of the country. The creek would probably freeze in the depths of the winter, but not so hard that horses or cattle couldn't

6

break through. Being a cattleman, born and bred, he appreciated this bit of land.

Still with a smile plastered on his face, he thought about his being a cattleman, one without owning a single head. Named James Buckley Armstrong by his father, and called Buck by his friends, he had grown up on a 1,000-acre ranch in the west Texas cattle country. He was a big man, standing an even six feet and weighing about 200 pounds, and there was something about him that caused careful men to take a second look. Even when he sat astride his horse anyone could see he was bigger than average. His habit of looking directly into the eyes of the person he talked to was, for some, disconcerting. With a strong tendency toward laughter, his deep-blue eyes seemed to take on a blackness in the rare times of anger. That was when careful men stepped quietly aside.

Buck was well-muscled, with little or no flab anywhere on his body, and his posture only enhanced his appearance. Even relaxed as he was, his erect bearing in the saddle made it obvious that somewhere in his past there had been military training.

A grown man of about thirty years, he was a wanderer with no ties to any land or livestock. That, he believed, was what made him a happy man, not having the grief and misfortunes that seemed to go along with owning land or stock. A fiddlefoot, his kind of stockman allowed him to travel from one adventure to another. However, feeling his stomach growl, he knew that even a traveler had to eat. With that thought, he urged his horse into a faster rhythm.

Upon rounding a large rocky outcropping he spotted the thin thread of smoke ahead. There, he thought, would be supper. He stayed close to the edge of the wide ravine and stopped the black when he came to a place from where he could look down on the depression and the rising smoke. Really not much higher, Buck sat and took in the working cowboys. A single rope corral held about a dozen head of range stock, horses of nearly every color but all at least two years old. Two men worked a small fire off to one side while two others roped a single horse at a time, bringing the captured animal to the fire.

Quickly and almost effortlessly, one of the hands flipped his lasso and caught the front feet of the roped horse. Jerking the catch rope he dropped the horse onto its side. Without hesitating one of the men at the fire was on the fallen horse, wrapping a sack round its head, blinding it. As they held their catch ropes taut, the horse was kept immobile. As the fourth man rushed from the fire with the red-hot branding-iron, Buck marveled at how well the men worked as a team. Only one rider, sitting his horse just outside the rope corral, seemed to be extra. He was, Buck figured, a young hand still learning the ropes, so to speak.

Carefully laying the hot branding-iron onto the hip of the downed horse, the man let it rest in place for a second, then, jumping up, he signaled to the rider holding the horse's head. In seconds, the horse was up on its feet and kicking a bit to show its displeasure at the brief pain. One of the mounted men quickly choused the newly marked horse into another rope corral beyond the holding-pen.

Buck sat his saddle and watched the operation. Once the horse was freed into the far corral, that rider quickly returned to take his part in repeating the action. Glancing up as he neared the fire, this cowboy was the first to see they were being watched. He let out a warning yell, pulled a rifle from the saddle holster and in one motion levered a shell into the breach, aimed up at Buck and fired.

CHAPTER 2

The attack caught Buck by surprise and the rider got another shot off before the big man could react. Quickly Buck reined around and kicked a heel into the big black's side. He leaned low over his mount's shoulder and quickly rode out of sight. When the firing stopped, Buck grabbed his own Winchester and left the saddle. He ground-hitched the horse and quickly ran back to where he could look down at the branding crew.

He poked his head around a protective boulder and watched as the men quickly tore the corral apart. The man closest to the fire had scattered the burning sticks and was pushing the hot irons into the dirt, trying to cool them down. Others were pushing the captured horses. A bullet striking the rock near Buck's head let him know that at least one of the riders was keeping a look-out.

Ducking back as another bullet whined by his ear, Buck chose another rock to look around. He brought his rifle up, levered a shell and, coming up quickly, he found his target and fired. Levering shells as fast as he could and still send them in the general direction of his attacker, he fired another half-dozen shots before dropping back out of sight.

Again from a new position, he looked down at the fran-

9

tic activity. Seeing two men, kneeling with their rifles aimed up the slope, Buck dodged back to safety. He placed his Stetson to one side, and slowly edged around the side of the boulder. Taking careful aim he shot at one kneeling man. The same one, he thought, who had opened fire on him first. Not waiting to see what damage he'd done, Buck swung his rifle and shot at the other rifleman. Bobbing back a second, he took a quick look just in time to see four mounted men, kicking their horses into a flat-out run, disappear into the willows. The fifth man lay unmoving near where the fire had been.

Buck leaned back against the boulder and took a deep breath. The battle hadn't lasted more than a minute or two but he couldn't recall having breathed at all during the excitement. Keeping one eye on the far curtain of green growth, he rested only to feel a sharp pain stab him in his left arm, up near the shoulder. He'd been shot and hadn't known it.

Checking once again to make sure the branding crew hadn't returned, Buck laid his rifle to one side and unbuttoned his shirt, pulling the bloody sleeve away from the wound. It hadn't been a bullet, the wound looked as though a knife had slashed him, ripping a deep cut just below the top of his shoulder. Quickly he removed his neck scarf and folded it into a long, thick pad. He pressed it against the wound, tying it as tightly as he could around his arm. Pulling his shirt up helped keep the pad in place. This would help slow the bleeding, he thought, but he'd have to find someone to look at it before it got worse.

First though, he'd have to try to find out why he'd been fired on. He reloaded the rifle from the box of shells in his saddle-bags and kept the weapon ready as he slowly rode the big black down to where the dead man was. His left arm was starting to throb and was stiffening, but if he had to he could use the rifle like a pistol.

Keeping an eye out in case the gang decided to come back, Buck circled a bit, coming onto the depression from the side away from where the four men had fled. For a minute he sat and looked around. Two irons, with their brands stuck in the dirt, stood with the handles sticking up. It was clear from the beating of the many hoofs where the small herd had been penned. This hadn't been the work of a ranch crew, he saw. He had come upon a gang of horse-rustlers changing brands.

Buck climbed down from the saddle and, keeping his rifle ready, knelt next to the man he'd shot. The man's nondescript clothes were the kind that any cowboy would wear: dirty and dusty denim pants, a faded cotton shirt and boots that were scarred and well-worn. Keeping the rifle handy, he went through the man's pants pockets. No letters or papers, only a few coins, and a two-bladed folding knife was all he found. A small beaded bag was in his shirt-pocket. Partly filled with cut tobacco, the bag was made of soft thin leather. Once the pride of some Indian woman, now dirty and worn from years of use, it only served to carry the man's smoking-material.

Buvk wrapped the meager belongings in the man's neck-scarf and stuck it all in a saddle-bag. Taking one of the irons from the dirt, he saw that they had simply the J shape on the end, typical of a running iron. In the hands of an expert, these could be used to make nearly any brand. Buck stuck the handles in the dirt next to the body so that anyone finding him would get an idea of what the dead man had been caught doing.

Back in the saddle, Buck took a last look around, then reined away. The ride back to the town of Jensen would take most of the rest of the day, he figured. From the directions his friend, Professor Fish, had given him, the fossil hunter's company should be closer, up in those dry brown foothills. He decided to trust to the professor's directions.

'C'mon, horse. Let's go see if we can find that bunch we're suppose to be looking out for,' he murmured, resting his left hand on his thigh to keep it still. As expected, the big black stallion didn't even acknowledge the words by so much as a twitch of its ears.

CHAPTER 3

A day or so earlier, Buck had ridden into town from the south. Stopping on a small rise he had taken a long look at the town laid out before him. It didn't look very different from any of the others he had ridden into, and out of.

A single main street was wider than most, but it was still simply a wide dirt track, a quagmire of thick mud in the spring and fall rains, frozen hard in winter months and thick with dust the rest of the year. A number of buildings lined both sides, most single-story with a few having a second level. False-fronts on many gave them the appearance of being bigger than they really were.

Gigging his black horse, he rode at a comfortable trot, crossing the bridge into town and noticing the clusters of structures lining a second rough street behind the main business section. These, he figured, had to be the homes of the business people.

One of the tallest buildings had a sign over the boardwalk indicating it to be a hotel; next door was a saloon. This suited the rider, a drink followed by a good restaurant meal and a feather-mattress sleep would take the kinks out of his saddle-stiff body. First step, however, was to stable his big black horse.

The black stallion and Buck had been together a long

13

time and got along fairly well. The rider had to be careful, though, to warn stable hands to keep their distance. The big black would bite or kick if someone he didn't like got too close. Other than Buck, there were few people the stallion liked.

Feeding his horse, paying for a room on the second floor and putting away a meal of thick beef-steak, cooked black on the outside but left dripping red in the middle, fried potatoes and two large slices of apple-pie, left the big man feeling pretty good. So good he thought he'd enjoy a quiet smoke on the hotel porch before having his drink.

Setting back in a wooden chair with his long legs stuck out in front, he rolled the quirly. He struck a sulphur-tipped match and fired the end. After a long day in the saddle, sitting and watching the early-evening traffic was relaxing. As the dark of the evening grew, fewer and fewer horsemen rode by. Buck's smoke was about burned out when three men came down the street and pulled in beside the hotel hitch rail. Buck frowned as his quiet was interrupted.

'What do you have against the Utah Star, Pa?' asked one of the riders, a young-sounding voice that Buck guessed belonged to the smallest of the three. 'It's certainly more alive than the Wilson's place.'

'That's only part of it, Jonathan. I'm here for a quiet drink before bed and being in the middle of a bunch of drunk, out-of-work drifters ain't my idea of pleasure.' Pa's voice was that of a man who had yelled his lungs out during many a cattle-drive, deep, rough and strong-sounding. It betokened the strength of a man used to giving orders and not having them questioned.

The third rider was a younger version of the oldest man, Buck saw as the three tied their reins and stepped up

14

on the broad boardwalk. Broad-shouldered and straight-backed, he stood quietly, thumbs caught in the arm-holes of a calf-hide vest, listening as the other two argued.

'You go right ahead into the Star if that's what you want, Jon,' the oldest man said, giving in but then backing it up with a gruff warning. 'But don't you go getting into any card-games and losing. You do, I don't want to hear about it tomorrow. And don't forget, we get our business taken care of and we're gone back to the ranch. I don't want to have to come looking for you, hear?'

'Ah, Pa, I ain't a child anymore. I can take care of myself. I'll be there for breakfast in the morning.' A quick nod to the silent one and he was gone through the swinging saloon-doors.

'Damn fool kid,' the oldest man muttered. 'C'mon, Cord, let's get our drink.'

Buck watched the pair walk down the boardwalk a piece before he got out of the chair. He'd finished his smoke but waited until the three men split up before moving so as not to intrude. Shaking his head at the age-old battle between a father and his growing-up son, he decided to follow the two men. A quiet drink was what he wanted, too, somewhere where he could sip his whiskey and think things over.

Nobody paid any attention to him as he pushed through the swinging doors of the saloon. Seeing a place at the end of the long bar that lined one wall, he settled in. The bartender was paying attention and was looking him over before Buck had gotten comfortable.

'And what'll ya have, cowboy? Our whiskey ain't watered and our beer is cool and frothy.' The barkeep was an older man, his once-white apron was tied high above a pot-gut and the traditional handlebar mustaches of a professional bartender hung well past the ends of his fat lips.

'A shot of your whiskey will start me off, I guess.' Buck let a silver dollar ring on the mahogany bar top. Standing tall he could look over the heads of customers standing alongside the bar. Most of them were leaning on their elbows, talking quietly to the man next to them, or simply staring into their drinks. He quickly spotted the two men just sitting down at a small round table.

Satisfied, he turned back and sipped at the whiskey the bartender had poured. Not the best he'd ever drunk, he decided; about what he expected. Now with one elbow on the bar he let his mind roam. It was the conversation he'd had with the professor that he wanted to study. He'd already gone over it a dozen times while watching the world go by between the big black horse's ears, but he still hadn't figured it out. As usual, the professor was asking if Buck would do him a little favor. It always seemed to start with a little favor but rarely ended up that way. But this time it really seemed to be a simple request for assistance. Would Buck find the time to help out a fossil-hunter?

That was what his old friend had said, a fossil-hunter. It wasn't often that the good Professor Fish asked for help, but when he did Buck couldn't turn him down. The debt he owed that man was almost too big and whenever the professor called Buck was the first one to put his hand up. But in the past it had been a matter of helping out some rancher friend of the professor, and once there had been the owner of a small stage-line that was being held up too often. Those were simple things to do, but helping out a fossil-hunter? Buck had agreed to do as the professor asked, even while not knowing exactly what it would mean.

Professor Fish explained that a man he had known at

college, a professor of natural history, was involved in something called a 'bone war'. Apparently Professor Andrew Cole had discovered a nearly complete skeleton of a creature that lived a long time ago. Somehow he had been given some money from the US government to go out and look for more of these skeletons.

All Buck could say was that it sounded like something those politicians in the nation's Capitol would do. Professor Fish didn't see the humor, so Buck didn't push it, and tried hard not to break out laughing when he heard the rest of the story. Professor Fish explained that another paleontologist had been jealous about Cole getting the federal money and was working to upset Cole's search. That search was to be for a bluff that someone had once seen, which was reportedly full of similar fossilized remains.

When Buck asked about what a pale-what-ever-it-was did, Professor Fish smiled and said he searched for bones. Bones of huge animals that lived millions of years ago, called dinosaurs. All Buck could do was nod.

CHAPTER 4

Fighting off a resentful enemy wasn't the only problem facing the good professor's friend, Cole. Even with governmental backing, no landowner wanted a small army of pick-and shovel diggers to come in and start digging holes. Especially as this part of the territory was mainly cattle-ranch country, and no rancher wanted strangers wandering around. That was where Buck's help was needed, trying to get the big ranchers to overlook the Cole exploration. Jensen, he figured, was a good place to start.

He finished his drink and motioned to the bartender. 'Tell me,' he asked, pointing up at the two men still sitting at their table, 'who're those two?'

'Ah, that's old man Calhoun and his older son, Cord.' The 'keep looked up and smiled, wiping the bar top with a piece of dirty toweling. 'They got the big spread out north and west of here. They're the biggest cattle-shippers in this part of the territory. Why do you want to know?'

'Oh, I just heard them talking with a young man before they came in here. Made me wonder.'

'That'd probably be Jonathan they were talking with. Jonathan Calhoun, Big John's younger boy by his second wife. His first wife died, oh, fifteen years ago, I guess. That one was Cord's mama. A few years later the old man went off and brought back his second wife. She already had a young son, Jonathan. Well, the two boys have been raised together and things have been good for old man Calhoun. That is until she died a few years ago. The boy took it hard and is getting to be a real worry for the old man, I hear. He likes to hang out over to the Star so we don't see much of him anymore. You want another drink?'

'Yeah, only I think I'll try your beer this time.'

'Good stuff, if I say so myself. That's 'cause I make it myself.' The 'keep laughed, causing his stomach to undulate.

'You own this saloon?'

'No. The fellow who has the general store back up the street bought it a couple years ago. We're not as busy as the Star, but then we don't have the poker-tables and gamblers here, either. This place is lot quieter, which is fine with me. What do you think of the beer?'

Buck sipped, leaving a white mustache of white foam on his upper lip. Wiping it off, he smiled. 'Real tasty,' he judged, bringing a bigger smile to the bartender's face.

Buck took another drink and glanced at the Calhouns. More than likely, the Calhoun ranch was just what the professor had been talking about, but he couldn't see how best to approach them about the fossil-hunters. If they weren't a problem, why start talking about solving one? Maybe he'd think of something in the morning. He waved to the happy bartender and headed back to his hotel room.

'Good evening, Jonathan,' the bartender in the Star greeted the young Calhoun. 'Come in for a few hands of poker?'

'Naw, I don't think so. Just a glass of beer. We've got a

19

big day tomorrow and I have to get up pretty early.'
Jonathan Calhoun was a slender young man. Dressed like
any working cowboy in work-clothes, worn denim pants
that had faded to a dirt-color and tucked into the tops of
stovepipe boots that were equally worn and scuffed. His
narrow nose hooked slightly over the almost non-existent
mustache that hung in straggly threads on a skinny upper
lip. A slightly fatter lower lip was made more noticeable by
the almost total absence of chin. Bright blue eyes flicked
as his long, nimble fingers closed around the beer-glass.

'Well, look who we have here.' A friendly voice caused
the young man to turn around.

Smiling, the young man nodded his head in greeting.
'Evening, Mr Henley. How're things going for you?'

'Oh very well, young man, very well indeed.' Motioning
to the bartender, Henley took Jonathan's arm and gently
led him to a table near the back of the long, crowded
room. 'I've got something to talk to you about, boy,' he
said. He pulled out a chair for the youngster before taking
another across the small table.

'If it's about that two hundred dollars I owe you, well,
I'm working on that. Honest.'

Henley laughed. 'Yeah, it's about that debt. But don't
worry about coming up with the money. I've got a little
offer to make that'll not only clear up that debt but will
leave a few dollars in your pocket, too.' He stopped talking
as the bartender brought a bottle of whiskey and two
glasses to the table.

Jonathan took a sip of the whiskey, coughing a little
when the sharp liquid bit into the back of his throat. Not
raising his head, he recalled the night he'd got into the
gambler's debt.

Since he was a boy wearing short pants he'd been

treated differently from his older half-brother, Cord, by the hands. Cord never spent much time in the bunkhouse but Jonathan, or Little Jon as everybody called him then, did. The hands, spending the evening hours playing poker, usually for matches, taught the boy the game.

One Saturday evening, a few weeks ago, he had come into town for the Saturday night dance held at the Cattlemen's Association hall. While Cord enjoyed himself dancing with all the women in town, Jonathan had been bored. After an hour or so, he wandered off and ended up having a beer in the Utah Star. There were few men in the Star, most being at the dance, and when one called over to invite the young man to take a chair at the poker-table, he decided to accept.

Henley had recognized young Calhoun when he walked in and after a few minutes he whispered to Stokes, the man on his right. It was Stokes who called out the invitation.

Jonathan took an empty chair, pulled a few bills from his shirt pocket and nodded his head. 'OK, Mr Uh, Henley. Let's see if I can make this into something worthwhile.'

Henley handled the cards with flair, shuffling and cutting the deck one-handed before passing them to the man on his left to cut. Slowly the game got started, each man playing cautiously, studying how the others played. For Jonathan, however, the play seemed to start off pretty good.

The first couple hands left Jonathan with a nice little pile of bills in front of him. Stokes played without seeming to look at his cards, while a shopkeeper named Holloway was more cautious. Taking one hand after filling a low pair and a lone ace with a second ace, Jonathan felt pretty good. Tonight just might be a good night, he smiled to himself.

When the next hand had been dealt Jonathan found himself with a lone king as the high card. No pairs or anything else to build on. For a time that was how the game went, no cards worth while coming his way. It was much later when the gambler, Henley, pulled a big pocket-watch from his vest pocket. 'It's getting on toward midnight. What say we play, oh, hell, let's make it two more hands and call it a night. That OK with everybody?'

'Yeah,' Jonathan said, putting his ante into the center of the table. 'The way the cards are going, I'm not even making wages sitting here.'

'You never know. This could be the hand that makes it all worthwhile,' Holloway said. The store-owner had played very conservatively, never winning or losing much, just enjoying the card-game.

Looking at the card dealt to him, Jonathan felt a thrill. Old Holloway could be right. A pair of deuces, a five of diamonds, a six of spades and a seven of hearts made the hand only one card shy of a straight. Looking around the table at the other players, he watched as Holloway tossed in his hand, leaving only Henley and Stokes to make their bets.

With the pot right, Henley called for cards. Carefully Jonathan pulled one of the deuces and threw it into the discard pile. 'One,' he said.

'And the dealer takes three,' Henley said, dealing himself the cards. Slowly Jonathan, holding them close to his shirt, spread his cards. There, the last one, a four of clubs. He had pulled his straight.

The bets were made and he'd won another game. Laughing, Jonathan pulled the pot in with a big smile.

'Now that's the way I like to see it. C'mon, deal them out so I can go home.'

Once again the cards were handed out and once again Jonathan found himself feeling a slight charge of excitement. Two pairs – sixes and eights. Making his bet, he tossed the odd card into the discards and called for a new one.

'Hey, isn't that what happened the last hand? You got another straight there, boy?' Henley asked with a laugh as he dealt the card.

Again, slowly and carefully Jonathan opened his hand. The sixes and the eights and, yes, he'd been dealt another six making him a full house. Hard to beat a hand like that, he thought, being very careful not to let the excitement show on his face. The others carefully looked at their cards and bet. Gradually with no one in a hurry, the pot grew.

'It's thirty dollars to you, boy,' Henley said, looking at Jonathan. 'Bet 'em if you got 'em. This is the last hand, remember.'

Jonathan looked at the pile of bills in front of him. This time he had enough. 'I'll raise the pot another five dollars,' he said with a smile.

Bet and raise, bet and raise, the hand was played out.

At last Holloway dropped out, leaving just Stokes, Henley and Jonathan. Henley looked over at the money in front of Jonathan and did a quick calculation. 'Boys, this is the last hand and it seems we all think we got winners. So, let's drop the limit. I'll bet a hundred dollars and call.'

Jonathan counted his bills. 'I don't think I can make it, Mr Henley. I've only got fifty dollars here. Let's keep it at five dollars.'

'But you think you have the winning hand, don't you? Tell you what. I think you're bluffing. I'll loan you the rest of the money to meet my bet.'

'Now, Henley,' Stokes said with a frown wrinkling his forehead, 'I ain't sure I can meet your raise, either. But, dammit, I got too good a hand to toss it in.'

'OK, I'll give you the same deal. I'll loan you what you need. Boys, I got a winner and I don't want to let it get away. What do you say?'

Jonathan looked at Stokes and saw the other man slowly nod. 'Oh, well. I guess you know I'm good for it. I'll meet your bet.'

Looking at his cards, Jonathan considered. A full house. Few hands could beat that and they certainly didn't come along often. It was the best hand he'd had all night and if he tossed it in, he'd be damn mad at himself. There was many times more than enough in the pot to make up for any of the losing hands he'd held.

'OK,' he said eventually. 'I'll accept and be glad to take the pot home with me. I got a full house . . . read 'em and weep.'

'Ah, damn,' Stokes said, tossing his hand unseen into the discard pile. 'He wasn't bluffing.'

'No, he obviously wasn't. But,' Henley said, his voice stopping Jonathan's hands as they reached for the pot of money, 'I've got a full house, too. Kings and a pair of nines.'

Jonathan thought his heart would stop. Two full houses in one hand. Who would believe it? All he could do was to watch as the saloon-owner pulled the pot toward him and started stacking the bills.

'Oh, hell, Mr Henley. I'll have to give you an IOU for the money I owe you. Will you wait until payday?'

'Sure, boy,' Henley said, looking up with a smile, 'but I don't want to take your paper. No, I guess we can work something out. Are you coming into town next Saturday night? Hey, we can have another game and who knows, you might win back what you lost. The cards, they come and they go.'

But it didn't work out that way. Still owing the gambler from the earlier game, Jonathan only got deeper in debt the next time. As he rode back to the ranch early on Sunday morning Jonathan's body drooped in the saddle. He was now in hock to Henley to the tune of $200.

'Don't let it bother you, boy,' Henley had said when Jonathan had tried to explain that he just didn't have the money he owed. 'What do you say the next time you come into town we discuss it. Don't let it worry you.'

But of course it did worry him. The loss was all Jonathan could think about and now, here he was with no money in his pocket.

'I watched your pa and your brother ride in with you. What'd they do, take their drink down at Wilson's dump?'

'Yeah,' Jonathan answered without lifting his head except to take another sip of whiskey. This time the liquor didn't seem to be so harsh-tasting.

'Well, that's OK for old people, I guess.' Henley chuckled. 'But let's talk about my plan. I've come up with a way to not only pay off that debt but to end up with a few bucks in your pocket.'

'What do I have to do, rob the bank?' Jonathan tried to keep from whining but knew he was failing.

'Nope. We'll just run a few horses from the far side of your pa's ranch into the Breaks. From there we can do some work on the brands and run them on to the railhead.'

'Steal from the ranch? I can't do that.'

'Why not? What did old John Calhoun ever do for you?

25

It was on his ranch that your ma died, wasn't it? Didn't you say that she might have been saved if the old man had moved faster? And what is it going to hurt? He'll never miss a handful of range nags. And that's about all we can move through that part of the country.'

'But what do I know about changing the brands? Hell, Mr Henley, I've never done anything like that before. I don't know.' Jonathan tried to keep his voice steady but the whine was loud in his ears.

'You won't have to have anything to do with the brands, or selling the horses, either. You know that area up there pretty good and once we've put together our little gather, why, you can ride on. I'll have the people there to take over and do the work of running them to the railhead. Then all you got to do is come into town and collect your share. Less the money you owe me, that is. Simple.'

CHAPTER 5

Buck took his time and enjoyed breakfast the next morning, a breakfast he didn't have to cook in a fire-blackened pan over a small fire. Outside he rolled his morning smoke and watched the morning stage take on its load of passengers and freight. Noticing the thinness of his tobacco sack he turned toward the general store. Typical of such establishments, the store had on its shelves and tables everything anyone would need or want, clothing, saddles, firearms, and canned foods and out back hardware such as nails and fence-wire.

Walking out of the bright morning sunlight into the warm gloom of interior, Buck slowed, letting his eyes adjust. A quick glance around ended at the sight of the woman standing behind the counter. Tall with long thick coils of sun-bleached brown hair that curled around her smooth face, her attention settled on the tall cowboy. Buck, seeing the display of tobacco and cigarette papers on a shelf behind her, stammered his request for a sack of Bull Durham. For a brief moment she didn't move but continued to look into his eyes. Buck was sure she was seeing everything about him, even what he'd had for breakfast. His smile relaxed a bit with that thought.

Neither had heard the door open or a third person

come in, until the man spoke.

'Is this jasper bothering you, Elizabeth?'

Buck turned, expecting to see a store clerk and was surprised to find a sharply dressed man standing a few feet away. Buck's first thought, seeing his long, thin face was that the man looked like a fox. Everything about the man was thin. A sharp nose separated from thin lips by a well-trimmed mustache had a small knob that indicated it had been broken at least once. His light-brown hair had been barbered and was shiny with some kind of pomade. Not looking down, Buck made a bet that the gambler's boots had been polished to a high gleam. A gambler, the cowboy thought; just like a proud bartender, you could always tell a prosperous gambler.

'No, Mr Luther Henley, this gentleman is not bothering anyone. He is a customer and I don't appreciate your concern.' She turned to Buck, smiled and quickly handed him the tobacco sack he'd asked for. 'That will be fifty cents, sir.'

Buck returned her smile, took coins from a pocket and paid. 'Thank you, ma'am.'

'No, I'm not anyone's "ma'am".' She looked over his shoulder at the gambler and added, letting her voice get a little louder, 'Nor am I anyone's woman to be protected.'

Buck laughed. 'Well, Miss Elizabeth, I won't say but it'd be a pleasure to be among those you called on if protection from wolves or,' quickly glancing back, 'any foxes was needed.'

That brought a chuckle from the girl. 'Now, if that's all, I had better wait on my other customer.'

Touching the brim of his hat, he turned, nodded to the gambler and strode out. With a new sack of tobacco, he decided to roll another smoke and was just putting fire to the quirly when Henley came out of the store and stopped.

'Drifter, that woman inside is going to be mine. I don't care to have you hanging around anywhere near her. It'd be a lot safer for you to just keep riding.'

Buck finished lighting his cigarette and turned toward the gambler. A leather strap across the man's lower chest indicated that Henley was wearing some kind of shoulder-holster. Buck had seen one or two of them in his travels, but had yet to find how useful they were. A good way to hide a pistol, he supposed.

'Well, Mr . . . what did Miss Elizabeth call you? Oh, yes, Henley. To tell you the truth it didn't seem to me that the lady is aware that she's to be yours. That, I'd say, leaves the door wide open.'

The gambler stood with his right hand resting on his coat lapel.

Relaxed while talking, Buck had let his right hand drop to the handle of his Colt. 'And if you move your hand any closer to that hidden weapon you got under that coat of yours, I gotta tell you, you won't make it.'

Shocked at getting caught, Henley's face blanched in anger. 'Damn you. This is the only warning you'll get. Ride on out of here. The next time you won't be so lucky.' Scowling he turned and stomped off down the dirt street.

Buck saddled up the big black horse and rode out of town, laughing when he thought about the gambler's anger.

CHAPTER 6

The professor had told Buck that Cole and his company weren't to know he was there to help them. Andrew Cole, he'd warned, was not open to having strangers around him. Seemed there was some competition in the search for bones, something to do with Cole's having won the government's funding or something. Fish expected that Cole would have hired a couple tough men to act as protectors along with his digging crew. Buck, being a cattleman of sorts, was to help out if there was any trouble with any ranchers, but leave the fossil-hunters mostly on their own.

With his wound starting to throb, he was pleased to find what he took to be Cole's party closer than he expected, only a few miles on up the creek that flowed down into the basin. Seeing the three wagons parked in a half-circle around a cook-fire, Buck reined in some distance away. Remembering that there might be some hardcases standing guard, he thought it would be better to announce his presence. The pain in his upper left arm had lost its sharpness and was now a dull ache. Any trouble from those in the camp would have to be handled without the use of that arm.

'Hallo the camp,' he called, then sat quietly in the

saddle: A tent had been erected between two of the wagons and from this a young woman emerged at his call. Two men, both dressed in dark-colored shirts and stovepipe denim pants with the legs shoved into the tops of their boots came up from the creek bottom. Both men wore gun belts, heavy with holstered weapons hanging. Carefully, Buck placed his right hand on his saddle horn and waited.

After a brief discussion the men and the woman walked out of the camp toward the mounted man. Buck watched as other men came up to the fire and watched.

'Good evening.' Buck nodded, slowly lifting his right hand to touch the brim of his hat to the woman. Closer, he could see that she was actually only a girl. She was pretty, with long brown hair held in place by a wide ribbon, her ankle-length dress held up from the dirt.

The men scowled and stopped, standing on either side of the girl a little apart and with their hands resting on the butts of their belt guns. 'What do ya want?' one asked, his voice low and deep, sounding as if he was standing in the bottom of a barrel. Both men were big, not so tall as wide, but stockily built.

'To tell the truth, I do find myself in need of some medical help. Seems I cut my arm and while usually I can take care of things . . . like pulling teeth when needed, or setting a broken arm, I've done that a time or two, this time I just can't take care of it.' He sat and waited while the two men completed their inspection of him.

'Well, land's sake,' the girl said, frustrated at the quiet reaction his words received. 'If you are hurt and need help, then get off that horse and let's see what we can do.'

'Miss Julie,' one of the men said, not taking his eyes off Buck, 'we don't want to be in any hurry here. Not until we know this jasper is alone and harmless.'

'Bosh. Of course he's alone. And he needs medical help. You heard him yourself. Now please stop playing bodyguards and let him come into camp,' she ordered, all of a sudden sounding like the one in charge.

'Ma'am,' the deep voice cut in, 'your pa hired us to keep March's men away. This here gent could be one of them. Now, I don't want your pa getting all het up 'cause we didn't do our job.'

Looking up at Buck, the girl asked, 'How bad are you wounded?'

'To tell the truth, I don't know. It's a cut on my upper arm, near my shoulder, and I can't see it all. It did bleed a bit, though, I can tell that.'

Nodding decisively, the girl took the big stallion's bridle and turned back to camp, leading the mounted horse-man, not giving the two men another look. Buck felt his face flush as he let the girl march his horse into the camp. His horse being under her control gave him an oppor-tunity to look over the men waiting by the fire.

The man in charge was clearly out of his element. Not a Westerner but, from his clothes, obviously a man of the big Eastern city. Brown leather flat-heeled boots encased his lower legs and the bottoms of his brown twill pants that ballooned out from the knee to the waist. His shirt was the same light-brown color and looked as if it had just come from the Chinese laundry, all hot-ironed with creases sharp and straight. Older, his hair was gray along the sides, melding into black. A thin black mustache sat neatly trimmed on his upper lip. Ice-cold eyes glared at the horseman being brought into his camp.

The other men, while not so well-dressed, were clearly from the big city too. Buck couldn't tell what purpose they served but it was evident that everything served the mustached leader.

'Julie, I hope you know what you're doing.' His words were as cold, as still, as his posture, not giving an inch even when speaking to his daughter. 'I had made it clear, there were to be no strangers allowed anywhere near our trek.'

His anger struck sparks with Buck. 'Hey, wait up there. I'm not someone you have to worry about and if you'll get off your high horse and let this lady fix my arm, I'll be on my way. I certainly don't want to be here any more than you want me here.'

'Stop it! Both of you! Father, this man is hurt and nobody is going to turn him away. He has nothing to do with your so important trek. He's just someone who needs help.' Turning to look up at Buck she gestured. 'If you'll get down, I'll get my aid kit and we'll take care of that arm.' She gave her father a last frown and marched around him, into the tent, her back as straight and stiff as her father's.

Buck swung down and stood by the black horse. After a moment, he couldn't help chuckling. 'Boy, with two stiff-backed Yankees in camp, this must be a fun place to be spending a quiet evening.'

For a minute nobody spoke. Eventually, with a big sigh, Julie's father let his shoulders sag. Turning back toward the fire, he stopped and looked back at Buck.

'Come on by the fire, young man. I guess she's right. I do get a little carried away with things. You have my apologies.' Motioning him toward a canvas-and-wood folding chair, he dropped into another. Buck looked the chair over and decided it would probably hold his weight. Sitting down gingerly, he didn't see the older man wave the others off.

'I'm Andrew Cole,' Julie's father said by way of intro-duction, putting his hand out. Buck took it and was surprised to find it work-roughened and strong.

'James Buckley Armstrong,' he answered. 'My friends call me Buck. I guess we got off on the wrong side of the saddle. I'll use the ache in my arm as my excuse for the bad manners.'

The girl came with her shoulder-bag and pulled another of the strange folding chairs up. With a pair of scissors she cut the bloody shirt away from his arm. The pad, also blood-soaked and stiff, was stuck to the cut. Pouring water from a kettle that had been sitting on a rack near the fire, she soaked the pad and slowly, gently, pulled it free.

'That looks bad, Mr Armstrong.' Cole grimaced when he got a good look at the gash. 'I think this calls for some-thing stronger than coffee.' He got up and stepped to the back of one of the wagons, where he dug around and eventually came back to the fire with a dark-brown bottle and two glasses. He poured the liquor and offered one to Buck. Julie continued to work on the cut and paid no attention to the men.

'Here, let's see if this will make things a little better,' the older man said, toasting the big cowboy. Buck looked at the light-brown liquor and smiled. The last time he had held a glass of good whiskey in his hand was so long ago he couldn't remember the occasion. Usually saloon whiskey was real rotgut, made on the spot and using a vari-ety of odd ingredients. Real distilled liquor was a luxury and not one to be hurried. He sipped and let the warming liquid melt its way down his throat.

So involved was he with enjoying the whiskey that he hadn't been giving any thought to what Julie was doing. A sharp stab brought his attention back to the injury.

'Damn!' he jerked.

'Oh, stop being a baby,' the girl said curtly. 'There was a bit of stone that I had to get out. I think I'm going to have to sew that gash up if it's to heal right. Am I going to have to fight you over that?' she asked. 'Or should I wait until you're drunk on father's whiskey?'

'No, you go ahead and do what you have to do. Just warn me that it's coming.' Whether from her jibe, the whiskey or maybe feeling a little fever from the wound, Buck felt his face become flushed.

'Stone in the wound? How in the world did that happen,' Cole asked, motioning to Buck to hold his now empty glass closer so he could pour more in.

'Well, I guess if you're anxious about visitors, you'd better know. I ran into a handful of bad guys back down the trail a piece. They were busy changing the brands on a small herd of somebody's horses when I stumbled on to them. Neither of us was expecting company, I'd say, but they reacted a lot faster than I did. One of their shots hit a boulder I was using for cover. That's probably where the gash came from. I thought I'd been hit.'

'Rustlers? We were told of a big ranch out here some-where, but I thought it was a cattle operation.'

'Yeah, that's likely. Even a small cattle ranch would have to have a pretty good-sized horse herd though. I figure they were just a few thieves taking advantage of livestock they came across. It's something for you and your company to be aware of. I left one dead, but four others rode away. They'll be around somewhere, I expect.'

'You killed a man?' The girl stopped abruptly and stared at Buck.

CHAPTER 7

'Well, yes, I guess I did. He was shooting at me and I didn't like it. It's something we don't care for out here, someone shooting at you.'

'Father, I've never liked the idea of you coming this far from civilization and now I'm sure you'll agree that we should turn back.'

'Now, Julie. We are here and the site can't be far away. With Harry and his partner we're safe. You worry too much.' He turned to Buck and shook his head. 'Ever since her mother died, she's insisted on protecting me. What she doesn't understand is, this is my life's work. I couldn't stop now if a whole army of rustlers came by.'

Julie reacted to her father's words by shaking her head; this was plainly a battle she had lost other times. She took up her needle and started stitching together the sides of the gash on Buck's arm. With the first jab of the needle Buck grimaced, but was careful not to flinch. Instead he took another sip of the whiskey.

'Uh, what exactly are you searching for out here, if you don't mind my asking?' Buck asked Cole, hoping the talk would take his mind off what the girl was doing.

'I'm a professor of natural history at Haverford College, just outside Philadelphia. Some time ago, I was fortunate

36

enough to be working with William Parker Foulke when he discovered a nearly complete dinosaur skeleton. That discovery changed my life. Paleontology has become my work. Finding and cataloguing the fossilized bones of creatures that lived here millions of years ago.'

Listening to the man didn't take away the pain his daughter was causing, but Buck didn't want to have him stop talking. Talking helped a little.

'Dinosaurs and fossils aren't something I know anything about. How do you find them?'

'Oh, they can be found almost everywhere, it appears.' Buck could see that Cole was in love with his subject. 'Why, archeologists have found evidence that primitive Indians used fossils, drilling holes through them, and might have worn them as jewelry.' Cole was visibly enjoying himself as he talked. 'People have been finding the fossilized bones of huge animals for a long time. This area is, I believe, rich in fossils and I mean to find them.'

'There,' Julie cut in, wiping her little needles and putting the tape and bandage material away in the canvas kit-bag. 'I think that'll help it heal. You should have a doctor look at it, though, first chance you get.'

From what Buck could see, the injury was already a lot better. Slowly he tried to raise his arm and felt little pain. The stiffness had for the most part disappeared.

'Thank you, Miss Julie. Maybe you should think about hanging out your shingle. If you can fix cuts and the odd gunshot wound, you could make a good living in almost any town around.'

'Guns? Does everyone have to live by the gun out here?'

'Well, yes, I guess so. Back in the cities there is organized law and police to keep the bad guys under control. Out here the hardcases have guns and most won't hesitate to use them to take what they want.' Buck heard himself lecturing the girl and stopped.

For a moment there was silence in the camp. Then Julie spoke. 'Father, I think it's time we got some dinner together.' Turning to Buck she asked, 'Would you care to join us, Mr Armstrong?'

Buck looked up at the sky and was surprised to see that the sun had gone down and night was closing in. 'Well, ma'am, I thank you. But I don't want to overstay my welcome. I can make a few miles yet this evening.'

'I wouldn't hear of it,' Cole announced. 'When you came into camp I was afraid you were from the March people. Now, I insist that you stay and have dinner with us. You can throw your bedroll over there and ride on in the morning. I insist.'

'Our cook puts out a quite good meal,' Julie said, smiling. Buck nodded and settled back in the chair.

'Who exactly is the cook of this outfit?' he asked.

'I am.' Julie laughed.

After a dinner of tender beef-steaks that had been pan-cooked in some kind of sauce, the men sat around the fire enjoying a last smoke and another glass of whiskey.

'Who's this March you mentioned earlier,' Buck asked.

Julie laughed and, kissing her father on the cheek, said she was going to turn in. 'I'll leave you two to your talking. I've heard all I want about the war between March and my father. Good night.'

'Now that really gets interesting,' Buck said, priming the elder man. 'A war between two men?'

Andrew Cole sat for a minute and then, staring into the fire, he started telling the story. 'Daniel March is professor at Yale College in New Haven. He came out to my digs in

Kansas. I had found another dinosaur skeleton and had a team of men digging it out of the marl, the rock surrounding the fossilized bones. March joined in and worked on the dig for two or three weeks. After he left I discovered that he had made a deal with many of my digging team. He would pay them a bonus if they turned anything they found over to him rather than to me as they were hired to do.

'That, I'm afraid, started it. We had an argument at the Academy and, well, we didn't part friends. Now every time I turn around there are people March has hired looking over my shoulder. He'll steal anything and everything he can and claim he found it. Sad, but not everyone realizes how crooked he is. I do apologize for my actions earlier.'

Buck made sure the other man was still looking into the fire before he smiled. Understanding the stress that this so-called war could cause, he was glad he'd be riding on in the morning.

CHAPTER 8

Thankful for the loan of a clean shirt, Buck saddled up and was gone before the rest of the fossil hunter's camp were up. Riding in the cool of the early morning was the best way to start a day, something both the rider and his horse liked.

'Now, horse, you have to admit there's a lot to like in this country . . . a pretty little girl that sews a nice stitch back there and another ahead in town seemed ready to talk. Yep, this is good country.' As usual the rider's comments were ignored.

Buck was looking forward to dropping down in that basin just further on and fixing his usual trail breakfast of bacon and fried bread and coffee. That was when he'd decide whether to ride back into town and report the shooting of the horse-rustler or to cut over to find the Rocking C and let the rancher, Calhoun, know about it.

As he rode down into the basin he found the decision made for him. Standing around the rustler's body were half a dozen mounted men. One spotted the approaching rider, and the waiting men all turned to watch him ride up. Buck pulled up a few yards away and sat returning their silent inspection. Three of the men, Buck saw, were the Calhouns, the eldest man in the middle with a son on

40

each side. The others, he counted five, were obviously hired hands. All were armed with sagging gunbelts and saddle-holstered rifles.

Buck judiciously let his left hand rest on the saddle horn, his right lightly on top.

'Morning,' he said, finishing his study.

For a minute nobody responded. Then, with a glance at his pa, Cord Calhoun nodded. 'Morning.'

Again nobody made any movement. Buck let a small smile play over his face. 'I guess it's up to me to open this dance, seeing as how you found some of the garbage I left behind.'

'See Pa?' the younger boy said, visibly agitated. 'He's got to be one of them. Ain't any other reason for him to be riding out here.'

'Whoa up, there, young man,' Buck said, holding up his left hand. 'Don't go making the mistake of bunching me in with anything.'

'You just said you'd been here and left this fellow behind. Can't deny that, and from the sign, those running irons and all, it's clear some brand-changing was going on. I say you got to be one of them.'

Nobody moved or spoke for a minute. Again Buck smiled at the young Calhoun. 'Nope. It isn't that clear to me why you'd jump to such a conclusion. And it could be downright dangerous to put the rustler label on someone unless you're mighty sure of your facts.'

'He's right, Jonathan,' Cord said softly. 'Until we hear this fellow's story, anyhow. How about it, stranger? What'd you mean, leaving your garbage behind?'

'I came onto them yesterday afternoon. Until one of them started shooting in my direction I thought they were probably ranch hands doing their job.'

'They shot at you?' John Calhoun asked disbelievingly. 'That's going to be hard to prove. Anyway, how come for you to come riding back here this morning? What'd you do, ride off and spend the night in a saloon somewhere and decide to come back to see what you'd left behind today?'

'Nope. They shot at me, I shot at them. Hit one, that one there, and the rest turned tail and ran. Somehow I took a wound in my arm that was bleeding pretty good so I rode to where I could get some help. Left that camp this morning and came by here on my way into Jensen.'

'Why go into town?' Jon Calhoun asked, not believing Buck any more that his pa seemed to. 'This is Rocking C land. You should've brought the news to the ranch. And what camp are you saying you found help? There ain't nobody camping anywhere out there.' He pointed with a sweeping of his arm.

'Didn't know where the ranch was. Still don't. But I did know where a party would be setting up camp.'

'Bosh, Pa. There ain't no truth in what's he saying. I say we should quit listening to him and string him up.' To Buck, 'That's what happens to anyone caught stealing our stock, stranger. That's what's going to happen to you.'

'Boy, you've called me a rustler and now you're calling me a liar. One of these days you'll have to eat those words. As for hanging me as a rustler—' said Buck, with no softness in his voice. Before any of the mounted men could react he had his Colt .44 out and aiming in their general direction, 'Then be ready 'cause I'm going to empty a few saddles the instant I think any of you're foolish enough to open this dance up.'

Cord Calhoun put both hands up shoulder-high and stepped his horse a pace or two out in front of the others.

42

'Stop. Damn it, Jonathan, stop that kind of talk right now before you get something started that you can't stop.' Looking at Buck, he nodded, 'Don't let him goad you, stranger. We'll listen to what you have to say.'

Buck slowly looked at the men facing him, each empty-handed but noticeably ready to pull iron. He nodded his head a mite, then let the .44 slip back into its holster. 'OK. I've told you what happened. Believe it or not.'

'You said something about a wound, didn't you?'

'Yeah, and it cost me a shirt. The lady that stitched up my shoulder had to tear my best shirt apart.'

'You left the branding-irons behind with this fellow's body. How come?'

'Now what could I say if your little brother came up behind me and found a couple running-irons in my saddle-bags? They're nothing to me, no reason to be carrying them around, is there?'

'Where were you headed this morning?'

'Exactly where I am going to go. I'm going on down the creek a ways, build a little fire and fix up some breakfast and then on into town to talk to the law and to get a new shirt. Now, if there are any more questions, you can either ride along while I talk to whatever law that's in Jensen or ask them while I fill my stomach.' He took the reins in his left hand and pulled, edging the big black horse back a slow step at a time.

'Hey, wait up,' Cord called. 'If you've got enough coffee for two, I'll go along.'

'Son,' John Calhoun barked, 'what're you doing?'

'Why, Pa, I'm going along with this guy. Have a cup of coffee and then ride on into town. I don't think he's lying and I don't think he's a rustler. Unlike some people, I don't jump to conclusions.'

'Wait up there a second, stranger,' the senior Calhoun called out to Buck. 'What about those folks you say are camped out? Any idea who they are?'

'Sure. A company of fossil-hunters, they said. Looking for a pile of fossilized bones from some creature that lived a long time ago. The leader is a man named Cole, Andrew Cole, as I recollect.'

'Damn,' Calhoun muttered, 'if there's something I don't need, it's a bunch of tenderfoot Easterners rummaging around the badlands up north. Boy,' he called out to Cord, 'you tell Butterfield that we're going to have a talk with them trespassers. That we're going to run them off.'

'I'll tell him, Pa, but it won't do no good. Didn't last time.' Together the two men rode away and were soon out of sight around the rock outcropping Buck had used for cover the day before.

Buck chose a place down the creek bottom a mile or so from where they had left Calhoun and his crew, a little flat spot in the bend of the flowing water. He and Cord loosened cinches and tied the horses to long enough leads for them to move around and select the best of the grass. Within minutes a small fire was blazing with a coffee-pot of water set to boil. Using the big blade of his folding pocket knife, Buck sliced a few rashers of bacon into his fry-pan, then, glancing up at the young man, added a few more. These pieces of cured meat and coffee would have to do.

Setting with his back against a small pine-tree, Cord watched silently. As was common for men riding the range, both carried their tin cups and a fork in their saddle-bags. After the coffee water came to a boil, Buck dropped a handful of crushed coffee beans in the pot and moved it off the fire to settle. When the bacon was cooked, he placed a few slices on a thick piece of pan-bread he'd purchased in town and handed it to Cord. After filling the cups and with his own bacon and bread meal, he leaned back against a boulder.

'Tell me a little about your pa's range,' Buck asked.

'He staked out quite a piece when he came into the country. I was just a year or so out of diapers to hear him tell it. Ma died on the trail and it was just Pa and me until he married Molly. The main ranch is over to the west and south. This piece is like a finger sticking up in the high desert country. The creek starts up north, there, and flows down to join up with the Red River. We don't run any cattle up here, use it mainly for a small herd of range horses and for deer-hunting. Keep it sort of private.'

'Seems the news about the fossil-hunters upset your pa a mite. Has there been trouble with those kind before?'

'Once, a few years ago. A bunch of Easterners came riding through the country telling everyone they were searching for bones, big old bones that'd turned into stone. That got a big laugh from folks, but nobody took them seriously until they cut a few fences and left a camp-fire burning as they moved on. That riled Pa and he took a few of the boys and chased them off his range. I expect that's why he got so angry hearing another group was coming close. He's a good man, just gets a little excited at times. He won't do much except rant and rave for a while. Sounds a lot worse than it is.'

Buck sat quiet for a moment. 'That's what I'm out here for, to make sure those fossil-hunters don't cause anyone any trouble.' He quickly explained about the favor the professor had asked.

Neither of the men spoke for a bit as he finished his meal. Cord watched Buck for a minute, then grimaced. 'I want to apologize for my brother's attack on you,' he said, pouring a second cup of coffee and settling back against the tree. 'He's usually not that quick to judge. Somehow, finding that body unnerved him.'

'Don't let it bother you. I expect he'll think a bit about his words and want to apologize the next time we meet. He's young, that's all.'

Letting the little fire bum down, the two men sat for a while. 'He's my stepbrother, you know. He was about 10 years old when his pa was killed. Pa married his mother and brought them to the ranch.

'That's when he took the wagon and rode out. He came back a while later and had a woman named Molly and her boy, Jonathan, with him. All he said was, this is your step-mother and stepbrother. Because Pa's name is John, with Jonathan we had two "Johns" on the place. Pa became Big John and we called my new brother Little Jon. For a while.' For a time Cord just sat quietly staring into the dying fire, remembering.

CHAPTER 9

For the most part, after a time of getting used to each other, life settled in for the Calhoun family. Molly turned out to be a good teacher, a good cook and up to the job of being a mother to the two boys. Cord was sixteen when disaster struck the ranching family again.

Rattlesnakes aren't born with rattles; those little warning devices come later. But they are born with a full dose of venom and a pair of tiny, very sharp fangs. Molly had gone for a walk up on the small hill behind the house. She didn't really feel the first strike on the heel of her hand and instinctively swatted at the second and third, thinking it was just some insect. Deciding not to fight the biting gnats or whatever they were, she headed back down the hill toward the house. She had just raised her hand to wave to her husband who, along with the boys was at the big corral inspecting a small herd of horses. Suddenly dizzy, her wave faltered and she crumpled to the ground. Cord happened to glance up the hill at that moment.

'Hey Pa, I think Molly just fell down. Up on the hill.'

'What?' John Calhoun had his mind on the half-dozen horses milling around the corral. 'What'd you say, boy?'

Little Jon had heard him. 'It's Ma,' he yelled, jumping off the top rail and running.

'Up there, boss,' one of the hands said, pointing.

Little Jon beat the others to his mother's side, but then could only stand there and look down at her. 'Help her, somebody. She's fainted.'

John knelt, turned her onto her back, lifted her head a bit and straightened out her arms. An older man, the ranch cook, was the last to reach the fallen woman. He went down onto one knee beside her.

'Boss, look there, at her elbow. There's a couple spots of blood on her arm.'

'That bug bite? That ain't enough to make her faint.'

'Somebody do something,' Little Jon said, his voice loud and anxious.

Cookie gently brushed one of the drops of blood from her arm and saw the tiny pair of puncture wounds.

'Boss, she's been snake-bit.'

'Gawd,' John said, his voice almost a whisper.

'Do something!' Jonathan wailed. 'Do something.'

There was nothing to do. By the time the men had carefully carried the woman down to the house, her face had turned pale and she had stopped breathing. Laying her on the bed, everyone could only stand back and stare. The only sound was the sobbing coming from Little Jon.

The cook put his arm around the shoulders of the boy. 'I'm surely sorry, boy.'

Looking up, Big John nodded. 'Son, I think we lost a fine woman.'

With tears streaming down his face, Little Jon threw Cookie's comforting arm from him. 'I ain't your son,' he yelled at Big John. 'You could've done something, but you didn't. My ma is dead and I ain't your son.'

'Little Jon. Of course you are. We'll get through this,

but we are a family,' Big John said, putting a hand out to the boy.

'No! And I ain't Little Jon anymore. My name is Jonathan. I don't want any part of your name. I don't want any part of you. Or you either,' he said, turning to Cord and the cook before running out of the room.

'Leave him go,' Big John said as Cord started after him. 'Let him grieve a bit. He'll come around once he cries it out.'

Cookie, nodding to Cord, quietly left the room with the boy slowly following behind. John remained, standing with shoulders bent, next to the bed.

The rest of the ride into Jensen was quiet with the two men buried in their own thoughts. The first stop in town was at the marshal's office, where Cord quickly introduced Buck to Mordecai Butterfield. Standing a full six feet tall, he was eye to eye with Buck. The lawman dressed just as any stockman, worn black pants hanging over the tops of his dusty, high-heeled boots and the matching suit coat just covering the heavy holstered .44 caliber Navy Colt belted to his waist. The shiny five-pointed star was carefully pinned to the pocket of his blue cotton shirt. A typical outdoorsman, the elderly lawman's forehead was white and almost pasty-looking from where his hat sat. Below that his sun-browned, lined face was marked by creases and age-wrinkles; some, Buck thought, were deep enough to hide a buggy in.

Holding out a work-roughened hand, Marshal Butterfield smiled. 'Well, I guess you can't be all bad if Cord here is walking with you.'

'That, Marshal, depends on what stories you've been hearing about me.' Buck's smile matched the lawman's.

'You might want to wait, though, until you've heard what I've got to tell you.'

Instantly, Butterfield's face got serious. He motioned to the two men to take chairs across the scarred wooden desk from him, and settled himself comfortably in a chair. 'I hope you're not going to spoil my morning, Mr Armstrong.'

'Well, if rustling horses out on Calhoun's ranch can do it, then consider it spoiled.' Buck then told the marshal about his run-in with the five men.

'Sounds as if you saved John Calhoun the loss of some range horses.' Butterfield nodded. 'And there was nothing in the dead man's pockets that gave any sign of who he was?'

'No letters or anything like that,' Buck answered. He pulled the kerchief-wrapped parcel from a back pocket. 'This is all I found.'

'Why, I've seen that tobacco sack before,' Butterfield said slowly, 'I just can't remember where. Cord? You ever seen it somewhere?'

'Nope. Hey, Buck, why didn't you show this stuff to Pa?'

'If you recall, those folks didn't seem too anxious to listen to anything I had to say. Truth to tell, I clean forgot it until we got to town.'

'Well, boys,' the marshal sighed, 'there ain't much that can be done. I expect your pa's buried the fellow, whoever he was, and without knowing anything about him there ain't much that I can do. As for the rustling, well, again, nothing to be done far as I can see. I suppose it happens at times, 'specially out there in the northern country where they ain't usually too many people around. I dunno, not much I can do.'

Knowing the marshal was right, Buck left the meager

personal belongings with him as he and Cord left his office.

'What now, young man? I'm all for a drink and then bite of supper,' Buck half-suggested.

'Yeah, I guess that's fine with me. I do want to stop by the store and see about a new hat. There's a dance coming up and I can't go bringing pleasure to all the local girls wearing a dirty, sweat-stained work-hat, can I?'

Remembering the pretty clerk, Buck agreed. 'Yeah, there's a few things I might need there, too. Say, what about that pretty store clerk? Is that the owner's wife?'

'Elizabeth Freeman? No, she's a widow. She's the daughter of the store's owner, old man Wilson. She married Matt Freeman a few years ago. He was a wrangler who worked for us breaking horses. A year or so ago, a horse rolled on him and crushed him. Her pa hadn't wanted her to marry Matt, said she could do better than a stockman. Now she lives in a little house here in town and works at the store.' Glancing sideways at the taller man, he smiled and tried to keep his question innocent. 'She'll be at the dance. You thinking about joining in?'

'Might. Have to wait and see, I suppose.'

An older man was behind the counter as the two men entered the store. Cord nodded to him and led the way toward the back where tables were piled high with men's pants and shirts. At the very back of the store, on shelves built against the wall, were stacks of hats, mostly Stetsons and mostly black, although some were a soft gray-looking, but all with wide brims that would protect the wearer from any type of weather. Cord slowly went through the piles until he found one he thought he might like. It was a flat-topped bone-gray felt hat and when he gently set it on his head he was pleased, as it seemed to be a comfortable fit.

Buck, remembering the shirt he'd need to replace the one he had lost when the Cole girl had patched up his arm didn't have it as easy. He had to paw through the entire pile until, down near the very bottom, he found one that would fit comfortably around his wide shoulders.

As Cord took the hat up to the counter, Buck was right behind him. Waiting his turn he noticed that the pretty clerk had taken the place of the older man.

'Good morning, Elizabeth.' Cord smiled his greeting, reaching for his wallet.

'Father just got those unpacked this morning. The price for that one,' she said looking at the little tag tied to the thin brown leather hatband, 'is twelve dollars.'

As he counted out the money Cord looked up at the girl's head. 'I'll be getting rid of that hatband and braiding one to fit. Until I get around to that, though, do you have any more ribbon like the one you've got in your hair?'

Shyly, she reached up and touched the light-blue ribbon. 'Yes. Let me find enough for your hat.'

She turned away, and Buck became conscious of a man standing to one side. 'Young man, I see the way you're looking at my daughter and I'll tell you right out. She is not for the likes of you. Make your purchases and then get the hell out of here and you don't need to come back.'

Flushing with anger, Buck started to turn, one hand already made into a rock-hard fist, but he stopped. The girl was his daughter. He couldn't very well follow his first reaction and lay the older man out.

Wordlessly the two men stood stiffly, taking each other's measure. Buck saw a small-built man in a white shirt and brown wool pants held up by a pair of black suspenders. Neither man spoke as the girl came up to hand the cowboy the ribbon.

'Here you go, Cord. That will be another fifty cents, please.'

Cord dropped a coin in her hand. He looked first at the smooth-faced girl and then, taking the ribbon said, 'Thank you.' Glancing first at Wilson and then at Buck, he started for the door.

Buck glanced over at the short man standing nearby and turned to give the girl a smile. 'Guess this shirt is all I need today, but I'll be by again, the next time there is a bit of ribbon, or the like, that I need.'

Putting his change in his pocket, he tipped his hat to the girl and, giving one more glare at the man still standing stiffly at one side, turned and followed Cord out of the store.

'Don't be hanging around, cowboy. I won't be giving out any more warnings,' the little man said to Buck's back.

'Father!' the girl said, stamping one foot angrily. 'You can't treat everybody like they were trying to kidnap me. I won't have it.'

'Yes I can. I won't have you getting friendly with any no-good cowboy.'

Outside Cord laughed. 'Boy, you do seem to rile people, don't you. Now you gotta go to the dance. It'll just kill old man Wilson to see you whirling around the floor with his daughter.'

CHAPTER 10

After deciding they would have a meal before bellying up to the bar, Buck followed Cord to the restaurant. Neither noticed a rider coming across the bridge and into town. Jonathan spotted them and quickly reined out of sight, going down the narrow street that ran behind the town's businesses. He tied his horse to the rail behind the Utah Star and slipped unseen through the back door. Seeing the gambler leaning against the bar talking to the bartender, he called out, keeping his voice low.

'Mr Henley. I got to talk to you,' he said nervously.

'Why, look here, Henry, it's young Calhoun. Come on in, boy, and have a drink.'

'No sir. I can't be seen here. I told Pa I was going back to the ranch, but I had to talk to you first.'

Motioning the young man toward a table against the back wall, Henley smiled as he sat down. 'Now what's got you so all fired up?'

'One of our riders found the branding-irons and the body of that partner of yours out in the creek bottom. He came in and told Pa and we all went out to see. Damn, I was sure I was going to get found out.'

'Now, why should you get found out? Mose was dead

and you didn't leave your calling-card lying around, did you?'

'No, but that hardcase that started shooting at us was there. I was afraid he might have seen me and would tell my pa.'

'The fellow that killed Mose? What the hell was he doing hanging around there?'

'He wasn't. He'd been wounded and had gone up the trail to some travelers he knew about to get fixed up and was on his way into town when he saw us all there by the body.'

'Who was it, do you know?'

'No. He said his name but I don't remember it. He's in town right now, though. I saw him and Cord going into the restaurant just now.'

'Cord? Why's your brother doing with him?'

'He ain't my brother. But I don't know. Cord didn't believe it when I tried to get Pa and the hands to think the stranger was one of the rustlers. I thought if they hanged him, or brought him into town nobody'd believe him if he did say he'd seen me. But that damn Cord wouldn't listen. When the stranger rode off, Cord went with him.'

'Well, I guess I'd better have a look at this guy. Now, you better get on to the ranch, don't you think?'

'Yeah.' But he didn't get up. 'Mr Henley, about those horses. We didn't get away with any so I still owe you that poker money. What're you going to do about that?'

'Boy, don't worry yourself. That's being taken care of. I'll let you know when and how in a few days.'

Not feeling any better, Jonathan left and, being careful not to be seen, headed back toward the ranch.

Henley took his hat from behind the bar, walked out front and strolled down to the restaurant. Walking by, he looked in the windows and saw Cord Calhoun at a back table sitting across from the big cowboy he'd run into talking with the widow Freeman.

'Damn,' the gambler mumbled to himself. 'What the hell's he doing, getting in my way?'

Upon returning to the Star, Henley sent Henry out to find Stokes. Something, the gambler thought, was going to have to be done about that meddling drifter and Stokes was just the man to do it.

After Buck and Cord had bought each other a glass of beer at Wilson's Saloon, Buck decided he'd spend the night in town, and walked his black stud over to the stable. Still talking about the day's events, Cord watched as the big cowboy unsaddled and turned his horse out into the stable's corral. Wordlessly they watched as the big black rolled in the dust.

'That horse of yours has a mean look to his eye,' Cord remarked.

'Yeah, every time I leave him stabled I have to warn everybody to stay away from him. He has a bad habit of biting or kicking anyone he takes a dislike to, and I'm about the only one he's ever liked.'

Laughing, Cord piled into his saddle, waved at his new friend, and headed for the home ranch.

After spending a quiet afternoon resting in one of the chairs on the hotel porch, Buck enjoyed a hot bath and let the town barber cut his hair and give him a shave before taking on the biggest steak the hotel restaurant could find. Later, leaning back in a chair on the hotel's porch with a five-cent cigar, Buck thought about the widow store clerk. Yep, maybe he had better get himself some clean clothes in the next couple days, just in case he decided to take in

Saturday's dance.

Feeling pretty good with the world, he stopped off for a couple drinks at Wilson's before turning in. It was while strolling back to the hotel that he changed his direction and headed for the stable, thinking he'd better check on his horse before turning in.

The old stable hand whom he'd warned about his horse wasn't anywhere to be seen, so the big man walked down the dark passage that ran the length of the stable. The black stallion was waiting for him as he came back into the fading sunlight, and allowed Buck to scratch between his ears. Having received a final pat, the horse walked away and the cowboy headed back toward the street and bed.

About half-way through the stable he stopped, thinking he'd heard something. He listened for a moment, then shook his head and continued. He was within yards of the street when they jumped him. There were at least two of them, one grabbing him from behind and the other swinging something hard against his wounded shoulder. It happened so fast he didn't have time to do much more than fall forward. Instinctively, he fell and rolled but the man holding him in a bear-hug hollered an order.

'Quick, damn it. I can't hold him for ever.'

Those were the last words he heard as a blow to the head sent sparks of flashing light behind his eyes and then everything went soft and black.

CHAPTER 11

Slowly, fighting to stay in the warm darkness, away from the throbbing pain that was just waiting, he came awake. Strange, he couldn't see and he couldn't move but whatever he was sitting on moved under him. Eventualy, pushed awake by the aching that beat like a drum in the rocking blackness, he realized he was in the saddle. Still unable to open his eyes, he tried to move his hands and, by feel, discovered them tied to a saddle horn. His legs were also bound to the saddle leathers. Listening, he didn't hear anything that made him think there were other riders nearby. Since he was blind and helpless, he hoped the horse knew where it was going.

Twisting his fingers, he tried to get a hold of the knots on the thin rope that secured his hands but couldn't. His eyes, he determined, were held closed by a tightly tied bandanna. Pushing against his shoulder to move the cloth was useless. Whoever had done this had done a good job. Too good.

Squeezing his legs caused the horse to stop walking for a few minutes, but when no other signal came, it went back to eating and moving.

Buck didn't know for how long he'd been knocked out but from the odors and what sounds he could hear, he thought it was now well after nightfall. He tried to remember about what time it had been when he went into the stable and recalled having enough daylight left to see his black horse. Something told him it wasn't his horse he was on now.

Thinking about who his attacker could have been, only one name came up. The list of people he knew in Jensen was short, the marshal, the store-owner and his widowed daughter, the bartender in Wilson's saloon, which brought up the owner of the Star saloon, Henley, and the waitress at the restaurant. None of them would have a reason to do something like this. As time went by, he racked his brain, trying to come up with an idea for getting loose.

Coming up empty, Buck caught himself dozing in the saddle. Then, jerking awake at one point, he started in again, trying to reach the rope holding his hands and, giving up on that, attempting to push the blindfold to one side. Another time the growing stiffness brought on by not being able to move woke him up. Once more he listened for some indication of what time it was or where he might be. A third time, when the horse stopped moving, he came awake. Probably the horse had dozed off. That time, when he moved his legs that were bound to the stirrup leathers, he kicked the horse causing it to jump and jar the hell out of Buck as it broke into a gallop. Soon though, the horse stopped and started chopping at whatever grasses it had found. Buck settled back and again dozed off.

As usual, Cord was up and had worked a couple hours swamping out the big barn before the cook rang the breakfast gong, which was actually the rusted rim of a small wagon-wheel hanging from the back door porch roof. Striking it let everyone hearing the noise know that a meal was on the table and when it was gone, there wasn't anymore until the next time. Cord washed up at the pan of cold water, dried his hands and face on a towel and found his seat at the big table in the ranch kitchen. He gave a general 'good morning' to those hands sitting at the table and a special nod to his father sitting at the far end. Jonathan had not come down from the upstairs bedroom, a habit that irritated the eldest Calhoun. Other than requests for the butter or some other item, the only sound throughout the meal was from forks hitting the plates.

Eventually, after emptying their last cup of coffee, the hands filed out to start their day, leaving only Cord and his father at the table. The cook and his helper quickly cleared the table and ignored the two men.

'What did the marshal say when that cowboy told him about the rustlers?' the old man asked.

Cord took his coffee and moved down to sit next to his pa. He shook his head. 'That there was nothing he could do. Not being able to identify the little bit of stuff Buck had taken from the dead man, Butterfield said he was helpless. The rustling, well, he figured the stock, being way out of sight of people, would be a good target for some enterprising thieves.'

'Damn. Well, I have to agree. They do pretty good back there, though, and we haven't really lost that many horses so I guess we'll keep them there until we need them for the fall round-up.'

Cord finished his coffee and sat quietly for a minute. 'What did you find out about the fossil-hunters? Were you able to find them?'

'Oh, yeah. There are three wagons this time. I talked with the leader; it's his show and apparently they got some money from the federal government to pay for the men and their equipment. The group is made up of old man Cole and his daughter and half a dozen men in all. Cole, it seems, is some high-level professor at a university back East. We had us a good long talk. Of course I didn't understand half of what he said. I still don't know why someone would come all the way out here just to look for some old bones.'

Cord smiled. 'I gather you didn't send them packing?'

'Naw. Hell, they ain't hurting anything. The places they want to look are over around the badlands. They said they'd be careful of fire and not leave any messes. Let them at it.'

'I'll bet Jonathan didn't like that. Pa, he's sure changed these past couple weeks. More than when his ma died. I just don't care to be around him any more.'

The elder man frowned, simply staring into his empty coffee-cup. 'I know,' he sighed, 'and I don't know what to do about it. Maybe there ain't anything that can be done. I just don't know. Anyway,' he went on, looking up at last, 'he wasn't with us. After you and that drifter left, he said something about riding back here. I saw him when we got in just before you came riding in. Haven't seen much of him since, though.'

Cord frowned. 'That drifter, as you call him, was asked to keep an eye on the fossil-hunters. Seems some high-powered friend of his down in the territorial capitol asked him to make sure they don't get into any trouble. Could be part of that deal the fossil-hunters have with the government.'

'Ummm, I don't know. They mentioned having sewed his arm up, but didn't say anything else about him. Which reminds me, that daughter of Cole's, now there's a young woman you should get to know. A real looker, and I got the idea she knows what's what. I'll bet she'd like to go to the dance next Saturday.'

'Pa, don't worry. Sooner or later I'll find the right girl and get married. You'll get your grandkids, don't think you won't. And stop trying to marry me off to every female that comes along. Now, there's some work that needs doing so I can't be sitting around here all morning chewing the fat with you.' He patted his pa on the shoulder, jammed his work-hat on and left the house.

Back in the barn he finished cleaning up the dirty straw and carried it in a big wheelbarrow out back to the pile of rotting material that had been removed from the barn over the past few weeks. He tipped it out, stood for a few minutes and, looking off into space, thought about what his pa had said. The fossil-hunter's daughter was a real looker, huh? There hadn't been a new girl to take to the dance in a couple years, since old Doc Frasier's daughter came back from nursing school. Then there was the fact that Buck had the inside track with the Easterner's company. Maybe, just maybe, the barn could wait. A ride into town just might be in order.

CHAPTER 12

Telling his pa where he was going, but not why, Cord quickly washed up again and, after changing into clean clothes, saddled up and rode out. Finding his new friend anywhere in town didn't turn out to be as easy as he'd thought it'd be. Apparently Buck had taken a room at the hotel but Wally Burns, the hotel clerk didn't think the bed had been slept in. Marshal Butterfield hadn't seen him, and the bartender at Wilson's could only say the big man had had a drink just about dark and had left.

It was finding the cowboy's big black horse still in the stable corral that caused the search to get serious. Talking to the old hostler didn't help any, he'd fallen asleep right after supper and hadn't woken up until the sun came up this morning.

'I saw him last night.' A young boy, barefoot and with both knees worn out of his pants was standing just outside the stable door. 'Course, I 'spect that information would be worth somethin', don't you?'

'What did you see?'

'Well,' the boy said slowly, looking down and studying his toes.

'OK,' Cord dug into a pocket and came out with a couple coins. 'Now, what did you see?'

With his eyes on the coins, the boy excitedly pointed down the street. 'He was drunk. Two of his friends had to hold him on his horse as they rode on outa town.'

'Drunk? The bartender said he'd only had one or two drinks. That wouldn't be enough to get drunk on. You sure?' Cord asked, holding the coins up.

'Yeah. Sure. Blind drunk and barely able to sit the saddle. His pards had to hold him or he'd've fallen for sure. Now, give me the coins.'

Cord dropped them in to his grubby hand. 'About what time was that?'

'Oh, just before dark, Thanks, mister,' the boy yelled, running off down the street.

Cord stood for a moment. That didn't make sense. If Buck had left the saloon about dark after only a couple drinks and the boy saw him a little bit later blind drunk, something was wrong. Then there was the fact that his horse was still in the corral. Something was very wrong.

He collected his horse and started riding in the direction the boy had pointed.

CHAPTER 13

The Red River started its meandering in the foothills of the Rocky Mountains, as a small stream coming from a couple springs and the melt of at least one high-peak glacier. Flowing south, it wound its way along, growing as more smaller creeks joined in and, because of the soil being washed along, started taking on its dirty reddish color that some early explorer noted on his maps. Long before reaching that part of Utah Territory where the community of Jensen was located, most of the redness had faded away, sinking to the river bottom.

For the most part, until reaching the narrow canyons farther south, the river was wide and shallow. Only in a few places was a bridge necessary, one such being along the northern edge of Jensen. Elsewhere travelers along the roads and trails simply forded the hock-deep, slow-moving stream. It was along one such shallow ford a few miles out of town that Cord noticed something out of the ordinary in the morning sunlight. The road was well-used by wagons and horses, the wheel-ruts and hoof-prints clear where the trail went. He'd stopped to let his horse drink from the edge of the river, when he noticed one set of hoof-prints wander off the beaten path.

He got down from his horse and felt the edges of one

of the prints. He determined that the sun hadn't yet had a chance to dry the thin dirt out. The horse that left that sign had done so after dark last night. He decided to ride along to see why.

For a mile or so the horse seemed to wander, first here and then there, with no real destination showing up. That wasn't the typical way a man would ride but was more likely a horse eating its way along. A loose horse this far from any ranch or homestead would also be unlikely, Cord thought.

The landscape was fairly flat with no rise high enough to be called a hill, but undulating, so that a horse could be right over there and yet out of sight. Following the marks left by the horse was the only way and that was slow going because most of the time the horse stayed in the high wild grasses. The sun was nearing its highest point when at last he came upon ground high enough to allow him a view of the next little valley. There, with its head down, chomping at the grass, was the horse. Slumped in the saddle on its back was a man.

Cord circled a little and came upon the mounted man from one side and slightly behind. Not sure whether it was Buck, he wanted to see the rider's reaction when he saw him come up. The young Calhoun almost reined in when he saw the rider's head come up at the sound of the approaching horse, but there was no change in his posture. Thinking it strange, Cord thumbed the thong off the hammer of his holstered Colt.

'Good morning,' the strange rider called out to him. 'Wouldn't mind giving me a hand here, would you?'

Cord recognized the voice. 'Buck? What the hell happened to you?' Kneeing his horse closer, he saw first the tightly tied bandanna and then the ropes holding

Buck's hands to the saddle.

'Well, I never . . . how did you get yourself trussed up like that?'

'Don't rightly know, to be honest. Don't happen to have a pocket-knife on you, do you? I'd certainly like to get out of this saddle for a few minutes.'

Cord reached over, pushed the bandanna off Buck's head, then cut the ropes around his wrists. Those binding his legs to the saddle leathers were cut away and Buck, sighing gratefully, swung down.

'You know, being in the saddle all day on a cattle-drive is one thing, but sitting in one place in that same saddle all night is something else. And that isn't even my saddle. Thank you, young man. I appreciate your timely arrival. I was thinking about chewing at the ropes when I heard you come riding up. But how did you come to be out here this fine morning?'

'Looking for you. Some kid in town told me he'd seen you, too drunk to sit your saddle, being helped out of town by a couple of your friends. Your mean black horse was still in the corral so I thought I'd better take a look. The rest is just plain luck. If I hadn't seen your horse's tracks leading off along the river back there, I'd still be going south and you'd be here making a meal outa some thin rope.'

Buck walked around a bit, loosening up his legs. The horse he'd been on ignored them both and continued chomping at the grasses. 'I can't believe that horse. He's been eating his way along since sometime last night and look at him, still gnawing away.'

Looking up at Cord, he asked about what the town kid had said he saw. 'That kid didn't say anything about the two who he saw helping me along, did he? I don't have any idea who they were.'

'Nope, he didn't say. All he knew was you were blind drunk and couldn't stay in the saddle.'

'Yeah, blind from the bandanna, but he was wrong – I couldn't have fallen out of that saddle if I wanted to, and boy, did I try. After I woke up, that is,' feeling the knot on the back of his head. 'They jumped me in the dark, in the stable after I was checking on my horse. I didn't see them and don't know why they were waiting for me.' Thinking about it for a minute, he frowned. 'No, they must have followed me after I left Wilson's place. Knocked me out and tied me to the back of that horse.'

'Hell of a way to wake up, I reckon. Tied to a horse and can't see where you are or where the horse is going. I notice they didn't bother leaving the bridle on the animal, so he couldn't step on the reins. Damn, you coulda ended up riding all the way to . . . I don't know what's on out that way. A long way to nowhere, I reckon.'

CHAPTER 14

Riding back into town, the two men took their time, letting Buck leave the saddle every so often and walk, letting his sore muscles loosen up.

'Wonder who I've made so mad?' he asked at one point, not expecting an answer. 'Hell, I haven't met all that many people in this part of the country. You and your pa and a few others like the bartender in Wilson's and that pretty widow in the general store—' Buck broke off. Then, 'Well, there is one man I've met who took a dislike to me. Yeah, and he warned me away from the widow, said he didn't want me bothering her. If he saw me in the store when you bought your new hat, then he could have made up his mind to do something about it.' Buck laughed. 'Maybe putting me on a horse to ride out of town was his idea of a joke.'

'Who are you talking about?' Cord stopped. 'Wait a minute. That gambler, Henley, has been paying a lot of attention to Elizabeth. Yeah. I wouldn't put some trick like this beyond him. He's a real snake, in my opinion. What're you going to do?'

Buck shook his head. 'I don't know yet. Something, though . . . you can be sure of that.'

Cord thought this was a good time to bring the fossil-hunter's daughter into the conversation.

'Pa said he'd had his talk with the fossil-hunters and chose to let them go on with their searching for bones.'

'Now that takes a load off my mind. I did hope that something could be worked out.'

'Yeah, Pa isn't unreasonable. It's just his way to some-times fly off the handle before thinking. Uh, by the way, he mentioned the guy who's leading that group has a daugh-ter. Pa said she's a real looker.'

Buck laughed. 'Yes, I got to admit, she has a nice way about her. Name is Julie and sews a good stitch, she does. What's the problem? Not enough eligible women in this part of the territory?'

'There aren't, and those that are, well, it'd be nice to have someone new to take to the Saturday-night dance.'

'Yeah, I suppose she would like to get out of camp and away from her father for a while. Is that why you came looking for me?'

'It's what brought me back to town. I wondered if you'd mind riding out and introducing me to her and her pa. I doubt if she'd want to go to a dance with just anyone that came riding up.'

Laughing again, Buck nodded. 'Say, now that gives me an idea.' Thinking about it for a bit, he chuckled. 'Do you think Elizabeth will be going to the dance?' When Cord nodded, he went on: 'Yep. I'll help you if you'll help me.'

With Cord's agreement, Buck explained his idea.

CHAPTER 15

When they came to the outskirts of town Buck left Cord and circled around, keeping out of sight. He found the black stud horse still in the back corral, next he found his own saddle and put it on his black horse. Meanwhile Cord had followed Buck's directions and, taking Elizabeth aside, asked her to attend the dance. Trying to keep his reasons simple, he found that the woman didn't have any questions once Cord told her the invitation was on behalf of the man who had been with him when he purchased his hat and the blue ribbon. She would be at the dance anyway, she assured the young cowboy.

Cord met up with Buck and his black horse on the other side of town. It took the two men most of the afternoon to find the fossil-hunter's campsite. After being introduced to Cord, Andrew Cole described how the search for the reported outcropping of fossilized bones was being handled. Buck and Cord listened and the younger man found himself interested and asking a number of questions. When the invitation to stay for dinner was given, both men quickly accepted.

After the meal, Cord's offer to help Julie with the dishes having been firmly turned down, the three men settled around the camp fire enjoying an after-dinner smoke and glass of the smooth whiskey offered by their host. Having finished the dishes, Julie joined the men, turning down her father's offer of a glass of the liquor.

During a quiet moment in the conversation Cord brought up the dance to be held in town on Saturday. At first, and before Julie could respond to the young man's invitation, Andrew Cole decided against it. His daughter, however, had a mind of her own. After listening to her father thanking Cord for thinking of his daughter, she accepted.

'Father,' she explained, speaking as if to a child, 'it has been nearly six weeks since we've been in a town. There are things we need from the store if we're to continue eating anything except rabbit-stew. Now, these gentlemen have invited us to a social function and I think we both deserve a night of relaxation. You can, and do, live for the finding of fossils. I, on the other hand, do not.'

Turning to Cord, she nodded her agreement. 'Thank you, Cord. We will ride in and do our shopping and attend the dance. Do you think there will be any ready-made dresses in stock at the store?'

'I couldn't say,' Cord answered quickly, not giving her father the chance to interrupt. 'However, you are about the same size, I'd say, as the woman whose father owns the store. Elizabeth Freeman is her name. I mentioned my plan to invite you and she asked me to tell you that if you wished, she could loan you one of hers, if necessary.'

'Oh, that would be wonderful. I wouldn't feel so, well, strange going to a dance and not knowing anyone if I meet her first.'

'You'd know me,' Both Cord and Buck said at the same time to great laughter from Julie. Letting his frown turn into a smile, even her father chuckled at the two men.

*

Buck rode to the Rocking C after leaving the Easterners' camp the next morning. He had dug out his best and cleanest clothes. With the help of the cook and a huge pot of hot water he got himself ready for the dance. Bootblack hid most of the scuff marks on his boots and made them look better than usual. A stiff brush brought out the best of his Stetson, although it looked a little shabby when compared to Cord's new hat, especially with the wide blue ribbon around the crown.

When it came time to ride into town for the dance, they were as slicked up as they could possibly be. Even John Calhoun had decided to go along. Nobody knew whether Jonathan was going into town or not until he walked into the kitchen and found Cord standing in front of the mirror in the kitchen seriously working at getting a comb through his hair. Stopping for a minute to watch, Jonathan decided to tease Cord. He had been jumpy and sullen since helping Henley with the failed theft of the horses, letting any little thing set him off. Maybe it was time to start laughing, he decided, before anyone got curious about what had made him so jumpy.

At one point, when that line rider, Buck, had come upon them out in the basin, he had been sure that the truth would come out. The next couple days he had been nervous, expecting at any time to have someone point at him and call him a thief. But as nothing happened, he settled down. The gambler had been right; nobody at the ranch would have even noticed the missing horses.

Now, a week or so later, it was Saturday afternoon and time to go into town, time to face up to the fact that he still owed Henley and find out what the man had in mind about getting paid off. Worried but not wanting to let anyone know it, he thought it'd be a good idea to joke with Cord a bit.

'Hey, Romeo,' he called out. 'Got a big night planned for town, huh? All duded up, clean shirt and, why, even polished up your boots some, I see. Who is the lucky girl this time? Not that new one over in the Pastime saloon, is it?'

'Nope. I leave those fast women to you. There are a number of other young ladies in town just waiting until I ride in,' Cord said, giving his hair one more pass of a flat hand and then centering his new hat, the one with the blue ribbon hatband, exactly so on his head. Turning toward the back door he continued: 'If you'd take some time away from that card-table in back of the saloon, you'd notice that. There are a lot of nice young women in town, and you could do yourself pretty good, if you wanted to.'

'Yeah, if I wanted to. But I don't. I like the action at that table. Better than sitting on some porch holding hands with some prissy little female who's just looking for a husband.'

Shaking his head, Cord walked across the yard toward the barn.

Later as the four rode in, with Cord and Jonathan ahead, the other two men talked.

'Wonder which young lady has caught Cord's eye,' John said. 'He's going on to the age to be looking for a wife, you know. Hell, I'd say I was about his age when I met his mother.'

'Whoa, old man,' Buck laughed. 'Don't be putting that cart ahead of the horse. Nobody said anything about marriage. I just said it's likely that Cord isn't blind or stupid. Anyway, the girl he's so interested in is part of

Cole's fossil-hunting deal. She won't be getting too far from her father, I'd think. Although you can never tell what a couple youngsters will do.'

John nodded his head in agreement 'Yeah, I agree. Jonathan now, well, that could be different. He spends too much time, I think, playing poker in that Utah Star. Doubt he really understands the kind of people he's playing with.'

Thinking about his night spent in the stable, Buck nodded. 'Well, a blind pig like that one can be a great teacher of boys, if they don't bite off more'n they can chew, that is.'

CHAPTER 17

The women living in town had one main night of social fun, the Saturday night dance in the Cattlemen's Association hall. Most of the men, all dressed in their cleanest shirts and with hair slicked back, spent the first half of the dance out by the horse-tie rail, sipping from various bottles of whiskey. Cord and a few of the other younger men stayed inside, taking advantage of the opportunity to dance with the women and girls. It was the one time they could meet girls of their own age and get to hold them to boot. With a fiddle, a jew's harp and a tub-strung bass, the music was fast and furious. Buck had arrived just in time for a song to begin. He stepped up beside Elizabeth and asked for the dance.

Cord was looking around the dance floor, but didn't see Julie anywhere. As he turned away he bumped into a soft body.

'Well, if I didn't know better,' he heard a soft musical voice say, 'I'd say you were trying to run from your dance partner.' The words were followed by a light chuckle.

Embarrassed, Cord found himself looking into the eyes of the girl he was there to meet. Flustered, more because of his clumsiness but partly due to the loveliness of the girl, he stammered, trying to get out some kind of response.

'Uh, no. I mean, well . . . I mean I'm sorry to bump into you. Are you all right?'

Once again the girl laughed as she answered. 'Heavens yes.'

'Would you care to dance the next one with me?' he asked, once again shy and a little anxious.

'I wondered if you were going to ask me, or if you were just going to stare at me the rest of the night. Of course, I would be happy to dance with you,' she said, somewhat formally.

Silence settled over the two as the first bit of embarrassment disappeared. Here he was with the girl he had come to the dance to see and he couldn't think of a thing to say. Sneaking a glance at her as they waited for the fiddle to start up, Cord saw that she was beautiful. Her long hair, more golden tonight than brown, was tied back with a sparkling white ribbon, leaving her face in full view. Her dress was a soft blue color, very close to the color of her eyes. A white collar ringed her neck and the dress outlined her breast before tightening around a smallish waist.

More to find something else to look at, he glanced around the room. 'Am I going to have trouble with your father if we dance?'

'I hope not. He's down having a drink with your father, but I expect they'll be along soon.'

Elizabeth and Buck were also discovering the fun of dancing. Slowly as the big cowboy lost his fear of stepping on the woman's feet, he started to relax.

'I seem to recall your father warning me to stay away from you. Am I going to have trouble with him tonight?'

'No. I can take care of him. He's just trying to protect me. He has the idea that only what he calls a professional man is good enough to meet me. I'm still very angry for the way he treated you the last time.'

Buck didn't respond and forgot his concerns as the fiddle started scratching out the next song. The big man didn't know it, but his face was almost shining with a big smile throughout the entire dance. Neither noticed the arrival of the girl's father, nor see the look he gave as he watched his daughter dance with the man he had warned off.

The rest of the evening went fast, too fast, Cord thought. Only once did Cord get hustled away for a dance with one of the town ladies. Hurrying back to Julie, he was just starting to make plans about asking her if he could walk her to her wagon when her father came up.

'That'll have to be the last dance, dear. We have a long ride back to camp and I want to get an early start on one section of the range tomorrow morning. Young man,' he said, turning to Cord, 'I thank you for inviting us to this social gathering. Speaking for myself, it was a good break, and I know Julie had a good time. Dear, I'll meet you out at the wagon.'

Slowly the couple walked behind the elder Cole, letting him get further ahead.

'I did enjoy myself, Cord. Maybe you can find time to ride out and visit in a few days?'

'You can count on it. We'll start gathering the cattle for the fall drive next week and I'll be pretty busy, but I'll find time to come out.' Quickly, somewhere in the dark between the well-lit door of the hall and the lantern hanging from the wagon, he leaned over and gave the girl a quick kiss. 'Good night, Julie, and thank you.'

*

Buck and Elizabeth had strolled away from the hall, taking their time walking down the street toward her little cottage. They stopped at the gate and, looking into her eyes, he bent his head and let his lips meet hers. Sighing, the couple parted and slowly, almost hesitantly, she pushed open the gate and, with a wave and a smile, went into her house.

The big smile on Buck's face disappeared and his hand fell to the cedar handles of his Colt as two men came out of the dark in front of him.

'Damn you, drifter.' Buck recognized the smooth voice of the gambler. 'I don't know how you got loose so quickly, but you should have taken that as a warning. Now you'll be sorry you didn't ride on. Get him, Stokes!' he yelled.

CHAPTER 18

Before either man could move, Buck had his six-gun out. Aiming at the dirt between them, he pulled the trigger. Cursing, the ambushers scattered, disappearing into the darkness. Laughing as loud as he could, Buck holstered his revolver and headed back to the main street.

Not wanting to push it too far, he decided to enjoy a drink at Wilson's saloon.

Luther Henley was fuming. Thinking he'd make a grand entrance at the dance, he'd dressed with extreme care. He was sporting a new suit, the whitest shirtfront made whiter by a brilliant red-satin bow tie and flat-heeled shoes he'd worked on with lampblack and wax to a perfect shine. As he walked through the Utah Star to his waiting buggy, which had been washed, the horse brushed and its tail braided with ribbons, the few customers were careful to hide their snickers behind their hands. Henley might look like a tenderfoot dandy, but the .38 Remington carried in that shoulder holster was no dude's weapon.

He'd planned on arriving a little late so that everyone would be on the dance floor when he walked in. The expected hush at the fine figure he cut didn't happen, though. Pushing through the door he stopped dead in his tracks as Elizabeth and the big drifter whirled past, her face upturned and smiling at something the cowboy had said. Stunned, he ducked back out into the darkness. Damn! How had the drifter turned up? Stokes had laughed with the telling of how he'd bundled the man up and left him. Damn that Stokes!

He whipped the beribboned horse back down the street, jumped down and, yelling for Stokes, rushed through the saloon, slamming the door to his office. He dropped into the armchair behind his desk and waited for his henchman to come in. Slowly, with a glass of whiskey in his hand, he started to relax a little. When the tall, lanky man pushed open the door and slouched in, the gambler was mostly over his anger and was thinking about revenge.

In a few words he told Stokes how his attempt to get rid of the drifter had failed.

'Hell, boss, there ain't no way he coulda got loose by hisself. I figured he'd be long lost. There ain't nobody or nothing out where we left him for maybe a hundred miles.'

'That doesn't matter. What does is what we're going to do now. You wait here. I'm going back to the hall. Somehow we'll get that hardcase.'

'Uh, boss. That kid is out front, Calhoun? He's standing at the bar and from the way he keeps looking back here, I'd say he's awfully scared you'll come roaring out, or maybe scared you won't.'

'OK. I'll be out in a few minutes. Buy him a whiskey or two and treat him gentle. I'll get rid of him and then later we'll take care of that damn fool cowboy.'

Henley ripped off the red tie and quickly replaced the new suit with his older, threadbare wool outfit. He changed into a pair of more comfortable high-heeled boots, made sure his shoulder-holstered pistol was in its proper position and went out to talk with Jonathan Calhoun.

'Hello, Mr Henley.' Stokes was right, the boy was almost wetting his pants.

'Hey, boy. How come you're not down to the dance? Lots of young ladies there, I'm told.' Henley, flashing a big smile, patted the youngster on the back. At a motion, Henry the bartender poured him a glass from the special bottle kept out of sight under the bar. Tasting the smooth liquor, the gambler let his smile grow as he turned to Jonathan.

'Now, what can I do for you tonight? Oh, yes. It's that gambling debt that's bothering you, isn't it? Well, I'm glad you're here. I've got something in the works that'll take care of that and more.'

'Uh, Mr Henley. I don't think I can go through any more things like we did last time. Anyway, the crew'll be out starting to push the stock into a holding-ground next week. There'll be hands riding all over the place.'

'No, we won't be doing that again. It's a sure-fire deal I've got this time. Can't fail.' He pushed another whiskey toward the young man's hands and watched as Jonathan took a sip.

'I don't know, Mr Henley. Getting mixed up in taking the old man's horses is one thing, but getting involved in something that could have the marshal out looking for us is something else. I think I'd better find another way to pay that poker debt.'

Shaking his head slowly, Henley frowned. 'But what would happen if someone, say Stokes or one of the others, let it slip about who was riding with that dead guy that drifter found?' Jonathan blinked. 'No, that isn't about to happen 'cause it won't be necessary. Relax, Jonathan, relax.'

Jonathan took a big gulp of the whiskey. Luther Henley smiled and patted the boy's shoulder again.

'Hey, boy. I'm in business to make money, not let anyone take it from me. But there is one way you can raise enough to pay me off and end up with a good chunk of pocket-money, too. And your brother, uh, step-brother just might end up taking the blame. What do you say?'

'Damn, I'd like to spike his guns. Everybody out at the ranch thinks his shit don't stink, but I know better.' Relieved after his scare and glowing from the whiskey he had been sipping, he felt his face flush. 'What kind of deal do you have planned?' he asked.

'Now it isn't all worked out yet, but it's a sure-fire job. Not any little penny-ante thing like taking a handful of horses to sell. But to make it work, to get Cord involved, you'll have to go back out to the ranch and wait for my signal.'

Jonathan let his head sag a little. Henley, aware of the whiskey the boy had been drinking, shook him a little. 'Listen to me, boy. You just get back out there. A few days, that's all. I'll get word to you and then you can simply ride out. There'll be enough money in this you can keep riding, if you want. Or not. Hang around and watch as things develop. You never know, you might end up back on the old man's good side.'

Shaking his head, Jonathan whined, 'I don't know I could do that, Mr Henley. I don't know if I could pull it off.'

'Look, boy,' Henley said sternly, 'you really don't have any choice. I need you for this job. Either you play along and do as I say, or some one will have a talk with the marshal. I'm sorry, but that's the way it is.'

'Ah, Christ. You really think I can get away with it?'

'Certainly, why not? Now, listen,' taking the whiskey from Jonathan's hand, 'you ride on back. Then, when the time is just right, I'll get the word to you.'

'You got me over a barrel. OK. I can try. But don't wait too long. There's a drive coming up in a couple weeks and we'll all be on that. Is that what you're planning? To take the cattle during the drive?'

'Don't you worry about it. Oh, and if you get a chance, is there anything of Cord's that you can pick up? Something that he wouldn't miss, but something that everyone would know was his?'

'Like what? I don't know. I guess there's something.'

'OK. You go on and ride back out to the ranch. Do your play-acting and be a good ranch hand for a while. I'll get a message to you when it's time. That's when you come for a night ride. Don't let anyone see you go or know you've gone.'

CHAPTER 19

Henley was right. Once Jonathan had returned, riding his horse up the road at a walk, letting his head hang down and keeping his eyes on the road ahead, everything went about like the gambler had said.

For the next couple days, work at getting ready for the coming round-up took everybody's attention.

Cord and most of the crew were out on the range, scouring the brush-choked gullies and hillsides for those older bulls and cows that were just naturally contrary. One by one the wily animals were roped and not so gently herded out to the holding-grounds. Once there it was the job of others to keep them within the herd. The plan was, once all the yearlings were branded and released, to shape up the herd that would be driven to the railhead. Only the young stuff, mostly heifers and a few of the slightly older bulls would be cut out to become the winter herd, to be kept over for another year or so.

Waiting for Henley to act was hard, and when Big John sent him out to work a distant area, he almost quit.

'I want you to go to work in that area out near the ponds tomorrow,' John Calhoun told him. 'Take an extra horse, 'cause it'll be hard going. I'll tell cookie to pack up extra grub, too, so there'll be no reason to come back in.'

Without another word, he turned to walk away.

Jonathan wanted to scream at the older man, but held it in. Yeah, he'd get his. Maybe not today or tomorrow, but sooner or later, Jonathan swore to himself, that old fart would get his.

With the promise of a hard day in the saddle coming up, he wisely headed for bed. Giving a wave to the old man and Cord who were sitting in the rocking-chairs on the porch discussing the round-up, Jonathan went through the house and down the hall to his room. He stopped at the door of Cord's room and looked back to see if the two were still at it. They were. Quietly opening the door, he glanced once more toward the front of the house and then slipped into the room.

The two boys had near-identical rooms, bedrooms they had had since either could remember. The old man's bedroom was off the front room and at the opposite corner of the house. Almost everything in both the back bedrooms was the same, a large down-filled mattress covered with a couple heavy wool blankets, one wall taken up by a wardrobe which held their few suits, hats and the odd pair of boots and against the other wall an unpainted pine chest of drawers. The only difference in the two rooms was the mirror that Jonathan had hanging over his drawers. Cord didn't have a mirror in his room. Instead, over the chest of drawers, was a set of deer antlers that was used as a hat rack.

Jonathan, seeing his half-brother's new Stetson hanging from one horn, walked over and quickly removed the blue ribbon that Cord had tied above the brim. He shoved the decoration into a pocket, silently reopened the bedroom door and listened. Hearing only the murmur of voices coming from the porch, he quietly closed one door, moved down the hall a bit, opened his bedroom door and went through. He didn't think Cord would notice the missing hatband. He wouldn't be wearing the fine new Stetson until the next trip to town and that wouldn't be until just before the round-up.

Jonathan didn't know what Henley had wanted it for, and he hoped that whatever the use, the ribbon hatband would do.

For the rest of the week, work on the gathering of a herd progressed at a good pace for the coming trail drive. All hands worked from can't see to can't see, either chasing cattle from out of the brush, working the branding-fires and holding the herd, or gathering and smoothing out the high jinks of the horse remuda. By the week's end, with another week left before the drive would start, everybody was ready for a day of rest.

Saturday afternoon, after bathing in the nearby creek and a big meal, most of the hands simply crawled into their bunks. At the big house, John and Cord spent an hour or so in the old man's office, recording the tally and planning the next week's work.

'How'd Jonathan do this week?' John Calhoun asked at one point.

'Well, I got to admit, he stuck with it. He'll never be a top hand but he can work when he wants to. I imagine he's just like the rest today, all the fight and bluster sweated out of him.'

'Now, you gotta get over it. He's just a bit younger-minded than you. He'll come round. Maybe won't make the hand, but what the hell, he'll do. You watch, he'll do.'

'Yeah. But I still feel there's something else going on under that hat of his. And I don't mean thinking about cattle.'

Shaking his head, John disagreed. 'No, I can't see it. He's taking care of that piddlin' little debt with the gambler in town, isn't he? He'll pay off that debt as soon as he can and that'll be the end of it, you'll see. He'll never have to know we know about it.'

With that out of the way, and the plans for the rest of the round-up made, the parley broke up and both men went their own way to relax, Cord to a shady spot along-side the barn where he rested and John to his rocking-chair on the porch. Neither man had seen Jonathan, leading a horse by the reins, slowly make his way out of the back of the barn and, wading the shallows of the creek back there, continue up the tree-covered rise behind. Not until he was a good distance from the ranch buildings did he climb into the saddle, and even then he rode slowly and quietly.

Just as Henley had said it would, the message to meet had come. Brought by Stokes, who had ridden in a round-about manner, unseen by any of the ranch crew, the message said simply to meet out by the Muddy Creek line shack. And not to let anyone know he had gone.

'Well, boy. I see you made it,' Henley welcomed him as he rode up to the cabin a little before dusk. 'Anyone see you go?' Just like when the gambler was meeting him to run the horses, Henley was wearing range clothes: worn denim pants and high-heeled boots, a sun-bleached cotton shirt and a cowhide vest. Around his waist, a gun belt held what looked to be a heavy Colt pistol in a leather holster. A near shapeless old Stetson, gray with years of dirt being worked into it by all kinds of weather, sat comfort-ably on the back of his head.

'Naw. They're all tired and most are already in bed for

the night. There won't be much activity around the place tomorrow either. That damn Cord is working everyone extra hard, getting the round-up done. What are we going to do?' Jonathan asked with a hint of excitement showing.

'Come on in and get a cup of coffee. We'll be leaving as soon as the others get here and we got some hard riding to do tonight,' was all the answer he got. Inside, with a cup of strong coffee in one hand, he asked whom they were waiting for.

'Stokes and two other fellows. There'll be five of us in on this.'

'It must be big, to make it worthwhile for five men.' Jonathan said doubtfully.

'Yeah, it is and don't you be worrying. There'll be enough so you can pay me what you owe and still have enough left over to have a whole handful of good times in town. Now, relax a bit till they get here so I don't have to go through it twice.'

Jonathan was almost asleep when, about an hour later, he jerked awake at the sound of riders coming in. He came to his feet and started to the door, only to be stopped by a word from Henley.

'Relax, boy. That's them coming in now. Come on, have another cup of coffee.'

Stokes and the others came in and, giving Henley and Jonathan a howdy, hurried to pour themselves coffee. Jonathan saw that of the five of them, he was the only one wearing clean range clothes. The others were all nearly identical in their worn pants, rundown-at-the-heels boots and faded shirts. Before he could comment on it, Henley motioned everybody to take chairs around the table.

'OK, now, this here's Jonathan and he'll be helping us in this deal. Jonathan, you know Stokes, and the other one's Jake and you remember Danny, don't you, from when we got run off on that horse-branding deal?'

The three men nodded their greetings.

'Here's the deal,' Henley went on. 'Jake and Danny have been scouting it all out. It's the stagecoach coming from Sedona on its regular run up through Jensen and then over to Silver Reef.'

'Hold up a stage?' Jonathan said, shaking his head. 'I don't know about that. We do that and there'll be all kinds of law out looking for us. I don't know if I like this, Mr Henley.'

'Boy, let me explain. First off, you don't have to like it, you just gotta go along and do it. Don't worry, once we're done, the law won't be looking for us. The way I got it planned, they'll be looking somewhere else.'

Without another word to Jonathan, Henley laid out the plan. The stage, he explained, would be carrying the payroll for the mining operations up north in the Silver Reef area. Nobody was supposed to know about it, but Jake just happened to work in the telegraph office in Sedona. He had read the message that'd been sent to the lawmen all along the route, warning them to pay special attention to that stage. Until the strongbox was dropped off at Sedona railroad detectives would guard it. Once on the stage, it would be that nobody knew what the box contained that would protect it.

Danny and Stokes, Henley went on, explaining his plan, had scouted the route and found the perfect place to stop the stage. It would be simple. They would just empty out the pockets of any passengers who happened to be on the stage and, with the strongbox on the back of an extra horse, disappear. To make it even harder for any posse to track them, Stokes had gone ahead and left extra horses in a couple stops. With fresh horses along the way, they'd be back in this area in time for Henley and Stokes to be at the saloon on Monday morning, and Jonathan back at the ranch. Jake and Danny would take care of themselves.

Looking up, Henley saw that Jonathan still wasn't convinced. 'Boy, there's a few other things for you to think about. This should bring us a lot of money. That payroll has to be worth more'n twenty thousand dollars. And one more thing, it won't be us the law'll be looking for, it'll be your brother.'

That brought Jonathan's head up. 'What? What'd you mean? Cord wouldn't have anything to do with holding up a stage.'

'No, I don't guess he would. But remember I told you to bring something of his? Did you?'

'Well, yeah,' Jonathan said, pulling the blue ribbon from a pocket. 'He used it as a hatband on his new Stetson. Everyone was teasing him about it when he put in on.'

'Well, that's it, then. The law will find this at the hold-up and after they lose our trail they'll go looking for him.'

'Hell, yes,' Jonathan added, getting all excited about it. 'The gather is getting down to the end. 'Most everyone is either all tired out and not noticing where everyone is or they'll be out trying to find the last of the herd. Just as nobody knows where I am, it's sure that everybody'll think good ol' Cord is still in bed. Whooie!'

'Yeah, I thought that'd get you,' Henley said, smiling. 'Just like that you get to pay what you owe me and at the same time, hang it all on that step-brother of yours.'

CHAPTER 20

Kelso Hale had been driving stagecoaches for almost twenty years and while there were times, especially on a cold winter morning, when he had more aches and pains than he liked, he was still one of the best at his job. This time, taking the extra pay that had been offered to run the entire 200-mile trip was easy money and only proved that others knew of his worth. Sitting high on the bench with the ribbons wound professionally through his gloved fingers, he carefully leaned to one side and spat a brown stream of tobacco juice.

Hale knew the iron-clad strongbox that was nestled at his feet was full of something of great value, probably more money than he'd see in a lifetime. Had to be a lot, otherwise the company wouldn't be paying Dusty Rhodes to ride shotgun. People like Rhodes didn't come cheap and men like him didn't take on a guard job very often. Usually, Hale knew, the black-suited whip-thin man sitting next to him was hired to wear a marshal's badge or carry the papers of a stock detective.

Sitting as comfortably as if on his sofa at home, the stage-driver was very conscious of the dusty, scruffy clothes he wore. Being on the bench with Rhodes made him feel like a bum. From the black hat hanging by the gunman's chinstrap to the black kerchief tied loosely around his neck, right down to the black shirt, pants and high-topped leather shoes, the man looked like someone heading for church or a funeral. But there he was, his well-dressed body swaying easily with the motion of the coach.

The only things Hale could see move were the black eyes that peered first here and then there out of sunken pale cheeks. Since climbing on board at the station in Sedona, the armed man hadn't muttered one word. Except for the eyes, Hale wouldn't know he was even alive. Ready for anything, he was, Hale saw, ready for anything.

Hale's job, on the other hand, was to keep the stage moving and his ability to handle the strung-out six-horse hitch was what he was being paid for. Except for the highly paid driver and guard and the strongbox, the run was just like any other scheduled run. That was the insurance, he had been told when offered the job. Nobody was to know that the stage carried anything other than ordinary baggage. That meant making the same few stops, picking up mail and passengers along the way. And keeping to the schedule.

So far, everything was going along as normal.

Not one sound was heard from the three passengers inside the swaying coach, but they lost no time in opening the door and going about their business once it stopped at the station in Jensen. Almost as quickly four new passengers climbed inside. Still on schedule, leaving town in a cloud of dust and with Hale's whip popping over the new team's heads, the stage continued on.

Further down the road, when the coach road started increasing in gradient, the incline was so gradual that only someone walking would notice, and then only after a while. Almost invisibly the road, in a series of long switchbacks, started up and then down a series of low-lying hills. Aware of the change in gradient and what it meant to the team of horses, Hale pulled back a little on the reins. This team had to last another twenty miles or so to the next stage stop at Zion.

Ever watchful, Rhodes increased his scanning of the brush and rock outcroppings along the roadway when traveling at this reduced speed. It was round one of the last switchbacks that Henley and his gang waited. The road had made a slight turn to the right, making it impossible for the shotgun guard to see the road ahead. A few large boulders had been pushed down onto the road, not enough to cause alarm, but enough to make it impossible for the stage to continue.

After stopping the stage, Hale sat for a minute, cussing at the job of having to climb down and roll the offending rocks off the track. Rhodes, ever wary, continued scanning the brush-covered hillside. Yelling for some of the passengers to help him, Hale eventually climbed down and walked up to the first of the rocks.

'C'mon and give me a hand,' he yelled once more to the passengers. 'If we're going to be on time, someone's gonna have to help out.'

Only after yelling the second time did the stage door open and two men come out to help. As they bent over to start pushing on one of the larger rocks, they jerked back erect as a rifle fired, followed by the blast of a shotgun.

'Nobody move, down there,' came a yell from the hillside. Hale twisted around to see what had happened to Rhodes, and saw the man slumped on the bench, blood seeping from a chest wound.

CHAPTER 21

'Now just stay as you are and nobody'll get hurt,' came the yelled orders from the hillside above the road. 'There're enough of us up here that you ain't got a chance, so don't be stupid.'

For another minute, no other sound was made and nobody moved. Then, slowly like ghosts, three men rose from behind bushes just off the edge of the road, all dust-covered, their faces masked by bandannas and each with a rifle aimed at those in the roadway.

'Now one at a time, starting with you, driver, pull any weapons you have and pitch them down off the road. Watch 'em, Buck.' The hidden gunman hollered. Scowling and cursing under his breath, the old stage-driver pulled a pistol from the holster on his hip and tossed it away. One after the other, as directed by the voice out of sight up on the hillside, the others followed suit.

At the orders from the unseen robber the other two passengers climbed out of the stage and were disarmed. Hale, given the order, climbed up onto the bench and took the shotgun and a belt gun from Rhodes. He threw them with the rest. He was then told to climb back down.

While the concealed robber gave directions, the masked men went among the passengers, taking wallets and watches. Then, to Hale's shock, they climbed up and tossed down the iron-strapped strongbox. The men scampered down and picked it up. Followed by the other masked robbers, they turned away and started walking down the road until they disappeared around the bend. For a moment nobody moved, then slowly, cautiously with one eye up on the brush-covered hillside, Hale made his way over to Rhodes's body.

When no more orders came from up above, other passengers came over to the driver.

'He's still alive but it looks bad,' Hale said. 'Does anyone know anything about stopping the bleeding?'

'I can pack it with a slip I have in my baggage,' the only woman among them said. While her bag was brought down from where it had been tied to the stage top, Hale cut open the wounded man's shirt. Quickly and firmly tying a thick bandage around his chest seemed to slow the seeping. Carefully moving the unconscious man, they gently placed him inside on one seat with his head pillowed by the woman's lap.

Before reboarding and picking up the reins, Hale, with one of the other passengers, climbed up the hillside looking for where the hidden man had lain. He had chosen a small rocky pile to mask his presence, leaving him a clear view of the road below. No sign of anything left behind was found.

The searchers were almost back on the road, when one of the passengers left at the stage called to the driver. That passenger, having given up his seat inside, had volunteered to ride on top. While the others were looking for traces of the bandits he had climbed on up on the bench. Now, calling to Hale, he was waving a blue ribbon.

'Hey, does this belong to you, driver?'

'What is it?' Hale answered.

'Looks like a wide piece of ribbon. It's been tied into a ring, like someone would for a hatband. It's too clean to come from your hat. I'll bet one of the robbers left it,' the man said excitedly. 'I found it kinda hooked on the edge of the bench there.'

'Well, give it here. I'm sure the sheriff in Zion will be pleased with it. Now, let's all get on board and get out of here. I'll take it easy as I can so as not to toss Rhodes around much, but let's get going.'

John Calhoun had decided late Sunday evening to ride out the next day and see how the round-up was going. It wasn't, he assured Cord, that he didn't believe that everything was being done, he just wanted to take a ride.

'Yeah, I understand.' Cord wasn't sure exactly how old his father was, he'd never been told. But he was of the opinion that the ranch owner was in his late fifties. Hell, maybe even older than that. The sun and wind had burned and toughened the old man's face and hands to a leathery brown. Simply owning the spread and being boss wasn't always enough and he was aware that his pa needed to feel a part of things.

'We'll be scraping the bottom of the barrel the first part of the week,' Cord had explained. Both men were at their usual place on the front porch, discussing the next day's work. 'I think we'll have all we'll get out of that brushy area down along Muddy Creek. We should be ready to head them out by mid-week.'

Big John was silent for a minute or two, gently rocking in the coolness of the evening. 'That'll work. I reckon the boys'll be ready for the end of the gather. They put in a lot of long hours last week. It's probably been good for both you and Jonathan. I haven't seen him since we came in yesterday morning. I'll bet he didn't leave the house and only got out of bed for a meal now and again.'

'Yeah, it's been quiet. Hell, even the boys down at the bunkhouse were pretty quiet the last couple days. They've been working pretty hard.' Both men were silent for a while thinking about what had gone on and what was left to do. Smiling, Cord looked over at his pa. 'You come on out tomorrow and I think you'll be happy with the size of the herd we got to drive to the railhead.'

By the time the old man had saddled a horse and ridden out to the big holding ground, most of the morning was gone. The crew had left just as the sun came peeking over the far hills and only the cook and his young helper, Freddie, were on the place to see him ride out.

Sitting his saddle on a slight rise above the herd, John watched as cowboys pulled branding-irons out of the small, smoking fires and branded the young stuff. Their bawls of pain and surprise were faint on the morning breeze. As he watched, riders slowly riding around the periphery of the herd contained even the rush of a big cow as she attempted to go to the aid of her just-marked calf. Cord was right, he thought, this would be a good-sized gather.

After relaxing in the morning sun, watching for a while as the work continued, he flicked his reins and turned back toward the ranch house. Keeping his horse at a walk and letting his mind roam, he enjoyed feeling the warmth on his back. When the first sharp pain struck, coming from under his left arm and quickly taking his breath away, he gasped and, hugging himself, folded over the saddle horn. Without thinking, he tightened his hold on the reins, stopping his horse. Slowly, as the pain spread down his chest and into his stomach, it lessened. Probably, he thought, as he relaxed his tightly closed eyes, he shouldn't have taken that last pile of bacon at breakfast.

Relaxing his hold on the reins and letting the horse chomp at the tops of the wild oat grass, the old man settled back in the saddle. This wasn't the first time he had paid the price for having eaten too much, or, for that matter, drinking too much. A few times recently he had suffered bouts of indigestion. He hadn't mentioned these to anyone; it was sure to worry the boys if they knew. Hell, they'd probably even start treating him like an old man. He wasn't ready for that.

But, he frowned . . . this time had been worse. Sure it was simply indigestion? He thought a bit and then decided that maybe he should pay the doctor in town a visit. Chuckling, he patted his horse's neck, more'n likely it was just a touch of overindulgence. What else could it be? Smiling to himself as the pain faded to become only a bad memory he once again flicked the reins, silently admitting that it was to be expected. After all, he wasn't getting any younger.

A short time later, still out of sight of the ranch house, his body was convulsed into a ball with another, sharper spasm. Losing consciousness, the rancher simply rolled out of the saddle, landing heavily on his right side. His horse, surprised at the sudden dismount, jumped a few hops before stepping on one of the dropped reins and stopping. Looking back at the man who had been on his back, he saw him lying unmoving on the ground. Not concerned, the pony returned to pulling mouthfuls of the sun-dried grass.

As he came aware, John's first thought was that he had

passed out and fallen off his horse, something he had never done even after the few times when he had taken on too much whiskey. His second thought was a silent cry of alarm. He was lying in the grass and couldn't move. Feeling panic, he pushed, trying to roll over onto his back, but still couldn't move.

'Lie quiet,' he told himself. 'Relax you damn fool. You can't do anything until you relax.'

Slowly, letting the wave of panic fade away, he realized that he was lying on his right side. He next tried to move his right arm only to discover that that arm, bent at the elbow, was being held immobile by the weight of his body. Tingling let him know the arm was asleep. His left arm, having fallen away from his body, simply wouldn't move.

Again panic welled up as he kicked his legs. He had to get free of whatever was holding him down. The sudden, strong thrust caused his body to roll, and he found himself flat on his back. It seemed to the man that hours passed as his arm, tingling painfully as blood rushed in, became usable. Letting the time pass as his body seemingly came awake, he took stock. He was on his back and could not move his left arm or leg. Flinching as a fly landed on his right cheek, he discovered that the left side of his face was also stiff.

Turning his head to the right took some effort but was worth it. His hat had fallen a short distance away but, he discovered, just out of reach. There was no sight of his horse and try as hard as he might, he couldn't hear the sound of the animal tearing at the grass.

For the next few hours the old man lay flat on his back listening to his heartbeat against the protective covering of brittle rib bones. The sharp pain stabbing him, at times like having a horse step on his chest, making it hard for him to breathe, had lessened, but it was certain to come back. John Calhoun was dying and although his mind yelled silently against the knowledge he knew it was so. Dammit, there were things that needed doing before he could give up. There was the ranch to run and his two sons to set straight. But maybe it was too late for that. Maybe he would die leaving his mistakes to live on without him.

Something bad had happened and he needed help. But nobody was coming to help him. Hell, nobody even knew where he was.

CHAPTER 22

It was dark when Cord and the crew returned to the ranch house. The day's work had gone well and from the low numbers of cattle that had been herded in, Cord could see that the end was in sight. They would be ready to head out for the railhead after one or maybe two more days of branding and cutting out the young stuff.

After washing up and changing into a clean shirt, he decided to take this news to his pa. He hadn't been in the kitchen when Cord had come in, and the young man thought he was probably working on paperwork in the office, a job the old man hated. Not finding him there, Cord headed for the cook shack. Maybe that was where John was, already down to supper. Usually, when the boys were there, the three of them ate up in the ranch house. John wanted the boys to feel that the big house was home and to remember all that Molly had taught them about eating like gentlemen. But often, when it was only the old man or when one or the other of the boys was absent, the others would walk down and eat with the men.

'No, boss,' Cookie said with a laugh when Cord asked. 'I ain't seen the old man since he rode out this morning.

I guess he was going out to give you a helpin' hand, huh?'

Jonathan, sitting at the other end of the long table and hearing Cord's question, looked up from his meal. Another hand spoke up, saying he'd seen the old man sitting his horse earlier in the morning, but hadn't seen where he went.

Worried, Cord headed out to the barn only to find that his pa's saddle wasn't hanging in the tack room where it was kept. Not seeing his usual horse in the big corral, he decided to saddle up and ride out. Jonathan and a couple others, having followed Cord to the barn, saddled up too, and went along.

Full darkness had come on and if there hadn't been a full moon the searchers would have not found the old man. As it was, what they found was the rancher sound asleep on his back on the east side of the slope of a small hill. If he'd been allowed to sleep the night away, the rising sun would have been sure to awaken him. As it was, the sun had done its damage. Without being able to reach his hat, the old man's face and forehead was sunburned a rosy pink.

Sending someone back to the house for a wagon, Cord gently woke the rancher up and listened while he was told what had happened.

'I just don't know, boy,' John said weakly. 'I guess that damn old horse spooked and dropped me on my back. I was pretty comfortable, so I didn't worry, just took a little nap.'

Cord, noticing how his father didn't even try to sit up, shook his head.

'Yeah, sure, Pa. You didn't break anything, did you?'

'No, I don't think so. I musta strained some muscles, though. I'm finding it a little hard, moving my arm and leg. Guess I fell on that side. I'll more 'n likely be all bruised up tomorrow.'

As gently as possible, with help from some of the hands, the old man was placed on a mattress of straw and blankets in the back of the wagon and taken back to the big house. Later, having been put to bed by Jonathan and Cord, he asked about the day's work.

While Jonathan went on his way to bed, Cord brought his father up to date, saying that the drive could probably be ready to start in a couple more days. With that report stopping any further questions, John nodded and closed his eyes. Cord quietly left the house and stopped by the cook shack for a delayed dinner of cold beef, thick sliced bread and hot coffee.

The next morning, after the big breakfast and coffee from the huge, smoke-blackened pot that was kept hot on the back of the stove, Cord had checked on the old man.

'Well, Pa, how're you feeling this morning?'

'Still stiffer'n a board,' John said, not moving much more than his right arm which was lying on top of the heavy wool blanket. Two thick and fluffy pillows were holding his head up so he could see who he was talking to without having to raise his head. That, he'd found out once everybody had left him alone last night, was something he couldn't do. His entire left side, from head to foot, was paralyzed.

'I wanted to stop by and see if there's anything I can do this morning. We're going to finish up the gather today and the branding and cutting out of young stock will be finished in the next few days. I think I'll stay out until we're done. I reckon we can get the first of the herd pointed by the end of the week.'

'Cord, you go on and do what you gotta do, and don't worry about me. I'll be all right. Ask cookie to bring me a small plate of grub, will you? And lots of coffee.'

With breakfast out of the way, and the cook and Freddie, his helper, busy getting all the supplies and equipment loaded in the old chuck wagon, John started working on his left arm. Just maybe, he thought, if he could exercise it, nobody would notice. For nearly two hours the bedridden man tried everything to get some movement in his arm. Even reaching across and picking it up with his working hand didn't help, he couldn't even make a fist. His left arm was as limp as a rag.

The old man had swung his legs out of bed and was planning on how he was going to limp out of the bedroom when he heard a horse come thundering into the yard. A yell from a deep voice as the rider came through the front door identified his visitor as Marshal Butterfield. Quickly, before the lawman could come into the bedroom, John fell back into bed and tried to bring the covers back up.

'What the hell you doing in bed, old man,' Butterfield asked, stomping into the room and stopping at the bedside.

'Good mornin' to you, too, you old bastard,' John said, but trying to smile left one side of his mouth feeling wooden. 'I took a little fall yesterday and tore a few muscles in my back. A few days on my back and I'll be all right. What are you doing out here this early in the day? I woulda guessed that you'd still be sitting in the restaurant in town drinking coffee, this time of the morning.'

'Ah, gawd, John,' the marshal said, not saying anything about the stiffness of the older man's face. 'I don't want to add to your troubles. But, well, do you know where Cord is? I gotta talk to him.'

'Sure. He's out working the gather. Why? What's happened that you need my boy?'

'John, I hate to tell you, but there's been a stage hold-up. Happened Sunday before noon up in the hills just outa Zion. A strongbox carrying twenty thousand dollars in payroll money was taken by at least five men. The hired shotgun guard was shot during the robbery and was brought on into town. He died a short time later.'

'Well, what's that got to do with Cord?'

'There was evidence left at the hold-up that points the finger at him. That blue ribbon he's been proud of on his hat. And one of the passengers said one of the hold-up men called another one Buck. That's that jasper Cord's been hanging around with. Dammit, that was the payroll for those miners up back of the Silver Reef area. As soon as the Zion sheriff notified the mine owners, here they come, a whole herd of angry miners. I got to get to Cord before they do.'

'Hell, Mordecai, you know Cord wouldn't have anything to do with any stage robbery. Someone's just blowing smoke, passing the blame somewhere it ain't.'

'John, you know Cord and I know Cord and you're right. But them miners don't know anything about him. And that store fella, Wilson? He's the one that named Cord. He's telling everyone that'll listen how a dirty cowboy was flirting with his daughter when your boy bought that length of blue ribbon. I got my horse and rode out here as quick as I could to warn you. They'll be coming right fast, I reckon.'

'Dammit, and most all the hands are out at the holding-ground. Well, they couldn't do much anyhow,' John said.

He watched as his friend went to the window and pulled back the curtains.

'Well, we'll find out. Here they come. Must be a couple dozen riders.'

CHAPTER 23

Hearing the group of riders coming into the yard, John moved as quickly as he could.

'Here, help me up. Dammit, Mordecai. I can't use my left arm or leg. I musta really done some damage.' For the first time, standing and being supported by the bed, John saw that he was wearing only his long johns. 'Ah, blast. Toss me them pants, will you? I can't go out there in just my underwear.'

As quick as possible Butterfield helped the stricken man into a pair of wool pants and a shirt. The marshal even had to fasten the rancher's gun belt around his waist. Together, the two men made their way to the porch as the crowd pulled up in front. While John leaned on a porch rail, the lawman made sure his badge was visible to the men.

'Where's your son, Cord?' one rider yelled out the demand.

'And what would you be wanting my boy for, stranger?' John asked, as he hitched his holstered pistol in a more comfortable position.

'Don't go thinking you're gonna run us off with that little pistol, old man,' the loud rider warned. 'And having the law stand up there ain't gonna help neither. We want your thieving brat and we're gonna have him.'

'Hey!' a voice behind the group of riders yelled out, causing most of them to whip around. Standing side by side and both holding shotguns were two men, one obviously from his apron a cook and the other his young helper, looking scared but determined. 'I'd think again,' the cook said, loud enough for everyone to hear, 'before I made tough talk to the owner of this place.'

'Dammit. It's this Cord that has our money and we're gonna get it back.'

'Nope, not as long as we've got these shotguns. They're loaded with double-ought buck and if you and your gang of hoodlums don't turn around and clear out, a bunch of you're gonna get hurt.'

'Boy,' Marshal Butterfield broke in, 'I'd suggest you all turn around and head back to town. I'm out here for the same reason you are and if John's boy had a hand in that robbery I'll be the one to bring him in.'

'Naw, we heard in town you're friendly with these people. Why should we trust you?'

'Yep, I'm friendly with half the folks in these parts and if I say I'll bring him in, I'll bring him in. But there ain't no vigilante crowd going to be part of it. If I need a posse, well then I'll appoint one, but it'll all be done legally and inside the law.'

The loud rider glanced around the clearly empty ranch yard and corrals. Then, seeing the pair of shotguns still holding steady, he nodded. 'OK. You're the law and we'll listen. For now. Howsomever, if you don't come riding in with that highwayman, we'll have to do your job for you. C'mon, boys. Back to town.' As he reined his horse around he gave one parting shot. 'We'll be waiting, Marshal.'

'John,' Mordecai said as they watched the miners ride

at a walk down the road, 'I'll have to do something. When do you expect Cord to come back?'

As soon as the riders turned, and the cook and his helper, with a wave, went back to the cook shack, John relaxed and leaned more on the railing. Seeing the pain this caused the man, Butterfield rushed to help him settle in the nearest rocking-chair. Wearily John gave his friend a crooked smile.

'Cord said he'd be back in as soon as the branding is done, a couple more days anyway. But Mordecai, you can't take him in. That gang'll get all whiskeyed up and you won't be able to stop them.'

Butterfield, shaking his head, frowned. The two men had been friends and had known each other for years, but now, for the first time in a long while, he really saw the rancher. Hair that was once black had turned mostly gray and the marshal wondered whether his own face had become as wrinkled as his friend's was now.

'John. I gotta do what I said. If I don't there'll be no stopping that gang. Until we get this straightened out, Cord'll be a lot safer in one of my jail cells.'

Sighing, John nodded. 'Maybe you're right.' He looked up at the marshal, his eyes tired and bloodshot.

'Look, I'll ride back into town and try to get a handle on what's happening. It'd look a lot better if, when Cord gets back, he comes in of his own accord. To make sure, you can have Jonathan and some of the boys ride in with him. I'll talk to the judge and see what we can work out. Judge Bell knows Cord and that'll help.'

'Yeah,' John said tiredly, 'I guess you're right. I'm damn tired. Help me back to bed, will you?'

A short time later, after stopping by to talk with the cook for a minute, Butterfield turned his horse back to town. There was more, he thought, to his friend's stiffness than tearing some muscles in a fall. Maybe he should send for that doctor and ask him to make a visit.

In the darkened bedroom, John tried once again to get some movement in his arm or leg, but stopped when someone knocked on the closed door.

'Yeah? Come on in.'

'Boss,' the cookie said, slowly opening the door and then standing there with the young helper looking over one shoulder. 'The marshal said for us to keep an eye on you. Said that you weren't feeling good and might need somethin'. Is there anything we can do?'

'No. Not right now. I'm feeling tired and think I'll sleep a bit. But thank you.'

'Boss, don't go worryin' about that gang of idiots. Ain't a chance that Cord'd do anything against the law. You jest rest up and I'll come back in later, OK?'

'Yeah and thanks, Cookie. And you too, Freddie. Thanks for coming up with those scatterguns. I don't know what woulda happened if you hadn't been there.'

'Ah, boss. We couldn't let them fellas yell at you like that, not on your own porch. You rest now,' he said. He pushed Freddie out of the room and carefully closed the door.

Lying back, unable to move half his body and a gang of angry miners out to find his boy, for the first time John Calhoun let the feeling of helplessness flow over him. Slowly, almost painfully slowly, he turned his head to stare at the belt gun that had hung from a bedpost. It had hung there unused for a long time. A reminder of his wild youth, he had taken it off the body of a man who'd tried to rob him when he first came into the country. The robber had been too slow and John had shot him with his old Remington rifle. Not owning a pistol, the young rancher had kept the old Colt .36 caliber five-shot revolver before burying the man. Reaching out his only working hand, he slowly pulled the long octagonal-barreled gun from its holster and looked at it.

CHAPTER 24

Julie Cole rode into Jensen the next morning in the company of one of the hard men her father had hired to act as guards. Wrapped in a sheet was the blue dress she had borrowed from Elizabeth Freeman. Sitting high in the seat of the wagon next to the driver-guard, the girl's eyes scanned both sides of the street, hoping to catch sight of Cord Calhoun. As they turned off the main street and stopped at her new friend's house, she sighed in disappointment.

'Oh, Julie,' Elizabeth exclaimed when she opened the door at Julie's knock. 'I'm so glad you're here. Come in, come in. We have to talk.'

'Why? Did something happen to Cord?' Julie asked worriedly.

'Not yet, but . . . he's being hunted by a gang of very angry miners and I don't think he even knows it.'

'What?' The younger woman was instantly frightened. 'Tell me, what happened?'

Quickly Elizabeth told her how the marshal had come back alone from his trip to the Rocking C and how the miners were outfitting to go hunting for both Buck and Cord.

'My father is handing out food and bullets to those

113

men, after making a big point of saying he just knew that drifter was a no-good. When I argued, Pa just laughed. This proved it, he said, no cowboy was good enough for his daughter and especially that one. I got mad and came home. I was considering getting a wagon from the stable and riding out to try to find Buck and Cord, but I wouldn't know where to look. What should we do?'

Julie thought for a moment and while Elizabeth made tea, she decided. 'I think I know where Buck's been camping. Cord has been working with his crew to fmish gathering for the drive. He stopped by our camp last night and told me they planned to start out in a day or two. He's so worried about his father. Apparently John Calhoun fell off his horse and hurt his back. Cord said he's bedridden. I was going to stop by their place on my way back to see what I could do to help.'

'How do you know where Buck's camp is?'

'One of our men said he'd seen the big man and his black horse out near the badlands where father believes the fossil outcropping is. Harry said as he was riding back that evening he saw a thin stream of smoke near where he saw the man earlier. Father thinks he's hanging around because someone hired him to watch out for us. At first he thought Buck was working for father's enemy, March, but not any more. He's been too helpful. I think it's sweet of him, to stay out of sight but still be so protective.'

'Does your father know a Professor Fish?'

'Why, yes. He and my father worked together on a project a few years ago. He's a wonderful man, older than Dad but a good friend and advisor. Why?'

'Buck mentioned being in this part of the country to help out someone, a request from this professor. Buck said he owes the professor more than he can ever repay. Do you think I should ride out with you and warn him?'

'No. If you go riding out your father or that gambler is sure to know you're on your way to help Buck and they'd follow us. Let me do it. I can have Harry ride ahead; he brought his own horse tied to the wagon. He can find Buck and I'm sure Buck will know where to look for Cord.' She put down her tea-cup and the two women hugged.

Instead of Julie and her guard finding Buck, he found them. Within a mile or so of where the fossil-hunter had reported seeing the big man on his horse, Buck came riding out from around a clump of juniper-trees and sat waiting for the wagon to pull up.

'Good morning, Miss Julie.' He smiled, nodding to the other man. 'And what brings you out in this God-forsaken part of the world?'

'Looking for you, Mr Armstrong. Do you happen to know where Cord Calhoun is today?'

'Yeah, I expect he's over yonder.' He pointed. 'His crew is about ready to start the drive. I've been thinking maybe I'd throw in and give them a hand for a few days. Things seem to be pretty quiet and this horse of mine needs some exercise.'

'Then you don't know about the stage hold-up.'

'Stage hold-up? Nope, can't say as I do. When did this happen?'

'There's a whole lot of angry miners who are coming out looking for you and for Cord. They want their payroll money that was coming in on the stage. According to the stagecoach-driver and a couple of his passengers, you and Cord were part of the gang that robbed him.'

'Boy, and here I thought things were quiet. When did this happen?'

'It'd be a couple days ago. Cord's father had his accident and the last day or two Cord's been out at something called the holding-ground.'

'What accident?' Buck could only sit his saddle and shake his head in wonderment as she told him all about John Calhoun's fall.

'Boy, it don't rain but it pours,' he muttered after hearing what the woman had to say. 'Tell you what, you go on back to your camp and I'll ride over to tell Cord he's a wanted man. I expect we'll have to hide out a while until the marshal finds who the real robbers were.'

He nodded to the guard-driver, who had sat quietly while the two talked, and gave an order. 'You see to her. Make sure she and her father are safe. I'll be in touch.' With that he lifted the reins and touched a heel to the black's side.

Finding the round-up crew was made easy for Buck by the big cloud of dust that hung over the ground ahead. He rode up and sat watching the activity until he spotted the young Calhoun. Reining in that direction, Buck was quickly spotted by a rider who said something to his boss. Cord quickly left what he was doing and rode out to meet the big man.

'Come out to see how the working class does it?' He smiled through dust-covered lips. Using his neckerchief to wipe the area around his mouth a little clearer, he held out a hand.

'I don't know if I should be seen shaking the hand of a wanted criminal,' Buck said, taking the offered hand.

'Wanted? Now who would want a dusty, dirty cowherder like me?'

'I'm told there's a whole passel of angry miners heading out in this direction. The story is they think you got something that belongs to them.'

Cord, seeing there was more than humor in the man's words, frowned. 'What exactly are you talking about?'

Buck recounted what Julie Cole had told him, all the while keeping one eye on the distant prairie. 'Now, I don't want to upset you any, but if I was in your shoes, and apparently I am, I'd be thinking about taking a quick ride out that way.' He pointed back the way he had come.

'Hell, man. I've got a cattle-drive to finish putting together. There's no time to go playing hide-and-seek with a gang of miners.'

'Well, that may be. But do you think those boys coming over there will take time to listen?' He nodded beyond the cowboys and their milling cattle. Looking over his shoulder, Cord saw a small dust cloud coming beyond the herd.

'Damn. Wait here a minute.' He spurred his horse and rode back to the nearest of his hands. He pulled up, the two men talked for a minute, then, having changed horses, Cord came galloping back. 'His horse is fresher than mine so we traded. Come on. We can figure out what to do later. Let's get out of sight before that posse sees us.'

CHAPTER 25

Keeping out of sight in the badlands was the easy part; not getting lost in the maze of canyons, ravines and dry washes was something else. Buck had located a small spring a couple miles up a gulch that was almost choked full of tall clumps of juniper and sagebrush. A low ridge on the other side of the campsite made a good emergency exit as it led deeper into the labyrinth.

'Hey,' Cord asked when Buck led him to his hidden camp, 'how'd you find this place? This is one of the springs we use as our base camp when we're up in the foothills deer-hunting. I didn't think anyone could just stumble on it.'

'I didn't stumble on anything. Just followed my stud horse. When he's been away from water for a time, he can sniff out the nearest mud puddle every time.'

They watered their horses and, having removed saddles and bridles, let them roll in the sandy bottom of the shallow ravine. Then the two men sat back while water boiled in Buck's coffee-pot.

Blowing to cool the black, steaming liquid, Buck filled in the other man with what he knew about the stage robbery.

'Seems the stage driver found something that puts your

name high on the list. You, or another of your gang, sang out my name while giving orders, so I'm on that list, too.'

'Damn. I don't understand any of this. I've been out with the round-up crew 'most every day for the past . . . well, since the dance, anyway. I've about lost track of days. Then there's Pa lying hurt in bed. Oh, damnation. I can't hide out here. There's too much to do.'

'Yeah. Plus I don't much like the idea of someone hunting me. What exactly happened to your pa?'

'I don't know. He rode out to check on the herd and didn't come back. We rode out and found him asleep on his back. Took him back to the ranch and put him to bed. He says he must have torn some muscles in his back, but I think there's more than that. I just don't know what.'

'Well, your crew can clear you. I've been riding around, mostly just me and the black horse. Haven't seen anyone since leaving town last Saturday night. Boy, was that a fun time. Hey, I didn't tell you, I even got to put a scare into that gambler fellow.'

'You what? Didn't you think he was behind your forced ride to nowhere?'

'Yeah. And I was right. He was really crazed when he stopped me in the street after I walked Elizabeth home from the dance. Him and one of his lackeys stopped me and he said he didn't know how I'd got loose but they were going to make up for it. Probably would have worked, except that when I pulled my Colt and fired into the dirt they seemed to change their minds. Guess I shouldn't have wasted that bullet, but I had to. It was just too funny.'

'You know, I think he's so anxious to marry Elizabeth because he doesn't like having her father's place compete with his Utah Star. Since he first came to town he's had to be the big shot, owning the biggest and best saloon. He even made Pa an offer for the Rocking C. An offer that was not even close to its worth, I'll add.'

Noticing the lengthening shadows, Buck suggested that they fix up a meal and bed down for the night. Tomorrow he thought he'd ride into town and have a talk with the marshal. Cord nodded in agreement, but said he wanted to ride in and talk with his father.

'Just make damn sure you're not seen,' Buck warned. 'I doubt that gang of miners would waste any time when you aren't able to produce their payroll.'

'And what makes you so sure they wouldn't be happy getting their hands on you? I'd say we're both riding soft and easy for a while.'

They split up the next morning, Cord wanted to ride over to where the Coles were camped to talk with Julie and Buck set out for town. He thought if he could talk with the marshal he could clear things up, or at least get his name off the most wanted list. If necessary, the Coles and their workers should be able to stand in his defense; he knew he'd been seen a number of times. Not knowing exactly when the stage robbery had taken place though, it wasn't a sure thing.

Riding at a steady trot in the early morning was one of the real pleasures of life for both Buck and the big stallion. The sensation was brought to an abrupt end when the black horse's ears twitched. Buck's right hand dropped automatically to his Colt .44. Looking ahead he quickly saw what had interrupted his morning ride . . . a bunch of riders heading right for him. Too late to duck out of sight, he reined away and nudged the black with both heels. A pack of men riding at top speed in his direction might not be the posse of miners, but he wasn't about to sit around to find out.

Keeping his horse at the distance-eating pace, he looked ahead for somewhere to escape into. The land, since he'd left the dry, erosion-cut tangle of gullies and ravines of the badlands, had fallen away, becoming mostly flat. Off to the left of the direction in which he was fleeing, the blue-gray of a mountain range hung on the horizon, much too far away to be of any help. Closer though, possibly within reachable range, he saw what appeared to be a series of low hills. Laying the reins on the side of the black's neck he changed direction.

The big black could run and hadn't had to for a long time, but even a high-powered racehorse could keep up the pace for only so long. Glancing back, Buck saw that the posse behind him had become strung out, some of the faster horses pushing well ahead of the main body. Faintly he could hear the yells as the leaders urged on their mounts. Keeping a watch on his pursuers, he trusted that the stud horse wouldn't step in any gopher hole. Seeing the leaders begin to lag, Buck pulled back a little on the reins, hoping to conserve his horse as long as possible.

Ahead he saw what appeared to be a break in the brown hillside and headed the black toward it. Getting closer he saw that a watercourse had cut through the soft earth, leaving a narrow ravine.

He dodged into the shallow opening and thought about making a stand, but decided there wasn't enough cover. Stopping now, he could hold off the crowd for a while, but it was sure that one or more would be smart enough to send a few men around and he'd be cut off. Slowing the black, he let him pick his way along the gully. Slowly, as the water-cut course turned, the walls, now high over his head, started closing in. Around a couple more bends and his stirrups were brushing the walls on either side.

Thinking he hadn't better get trapped, he was almost to the point of turning back when the sandy bottom started to rise. When the horse started slipping in the thick sand, Buck swung down, and leading the animal by the reins, climbed the incline. As he came to a fork he could see that in one direction the water channel narrowed and disappeared. During the storm that gave birth to this culvert, that would have been a waterfall. Not seeing any defensible position, he turned the other way. Shade gave way to sunlight as the watercourse rose. Abruptly Buck found himself up on a flat bluff. Standing quietly, he looked down over the flat area he'd just been chased over. No sound came from up the draw he'd just climbed, but he doubted if the miners had given up. Sooner or later they'd be coming.

Back in the saddle he searched for a place to hide. Flat as a table, only random clumps of sagebrush broke the landscape as far as he could see. Looking back at the ravine, he thought about it for a minute, then took his rifle from the saddle holster and ground-hitched his horse. Maybe he could put a little scare in the men behind him. If nothing else, it'd give his horse a breather.

He walked a short distance along the edge of the draw until he found a place from where he could look down on the fork. Lying on his stomach on a shady patch of sand to the side of a Juniper tree, he aimed his fully loaded Winchester lever-action rifle on the trail below. In the past this rifle had brought down its share of deer, but today there would be a different target. This time he would have to choose his victim well; unlike the deer, these could shoot back.

The kind of silence found only in dry desert areas had

settled in, and Buck, totally relaxed in the stillness, was beginning to wonder where the miners had gone when the first noise brought him alert. As the sound of men talking and horse-gear creaking came echoing up the draw, Buck checked the rifle's safety. As the first of the riders came into view he took careful aim at the first man in line. Aiming slightly ahead of the man, and taking up the slack of the trigger, he was mildly surprised when the gun fired. The cowboy below left the saddle as if shot, landing on his back. Scrambling up he half-ran and half-fell back out of sight.

These men might have blood in their eyes, but he couldn't just shoot them from ambush. That warning shot, he hoped, would send them on their way.

For a brief time nothing was heard, and then in a burst of horses, a half-dozen riders came barreling into sight, all firing their weapons up in the direction they thought the hidden sniper was, hoping for a lucky shot. None of the bullets came anywhere close to Buck. Taking his time, he carefully aimed and fired, hitting one man in the shoulder before swinging to shoot at another. As the riders scattered, he fired shot after shot at them, not taking time to aim, and sending most of his bullets into the wall behind them. The noise of the gunfire and the bursts of sand hitting them on the head panicked the riders as well as the horses. With yells the men tried to duck back out of danger, pulling the wounded men with them.

Figuring it would take them a while to get up the nerve to try it again, Buck reloaded the rifle and scrambled back to his horse. He climbed into the saddle and rode at a walk out onto the flats. Somewhere he'd have to find a safe place, a place with water.

CHAPTER 26

Cord's visit with Julie and her father was cordial but not very satisfying. Julie's father was excited about some large rocks one of his crew had brought in and the girl was kept busy taking notes as parts of the rocks were measured and picked at. The rocks, as far as Cord could see, were just like any other, but the interest shown by everyone in the camp was amazing. Feeling out of place, he left after only a brief visit and, keeping below the skyline where possible, took a long way around to the Rocking C headquarters.

Jonathan couldn't believe it when Cord came out of the barn and into the house the next evening.

'What the . . . what are you doing here, Cord?' he stammered. 'Half the county is out looking for you. The marshal's been out talking to Pa at least once a day. He was here earlier and left just before supper. I figure he's checking to see if you show up, and he was right. Here you are. Boy, if any of those miners get their hands on you, you'll wish they hadn't.'

'Yeah, and hello to you, too. I came in through the barn

and waited until almost dark so nobody'd see me. I gotta see Pa. How is he?'

'As mean-mouthed as ever. Hurting, I'd say.'

'Pa must be in some pain if he's talking mean. I'll go in and see him.'

'Yeah, you do that. Me, I'm heading for town. With the old man flat on his back, he can't keep me on the ranch.'

'Well, make sure you don't say anything to your friends about seeing me.'

'Of course not. What do you take me for?'

'Sometimes I wonder,' Cord said. He left the room and headed to his pa's bedroom.

Slipping into the room as quietly as he could, Cord looked down at his pa and was surprised at how old he looked. Tired and even thinner than he'd been just a couple days ago. Cord looked around, spotted a chair and pulled it back to the bedside to find himself staring into the black cave of a gun barrel.

'Shouldn't sneak up on a man, son,' John Calhoun said, slipping the long-barreled firearm back under the blankets. 'What're you doing here? Didn't someone warn you to stay away? For sure there's a couple of them miners out there watching the house.'

'Yeah, I figured they'd be so I waited until it was mostly dark and then I came in through the barn. I had to come talk to you, see how you're doing.'

'Well, there's still some stiffness, but resting is helping. I'm feeling better. Most likely be up and back in the saddle in a couple days.'

'I don't know, Pa. You look like you haven't been sleeping very much. Is Cookie bringing your food?'

'Yeah. They're taking good care of me. Almost too good. Just don't seem to have any time to myself, what with Cookie coming in at all hours and then the marshal. He's some worried about you. He'll be madder'n hell when he hears you came in. Dammit, boy, you gotta get back outa sight. Get out in the badlands and stay there.'

Both men jumped when the bedroom door opened, only to relax when Cookie came through. 'Boy, you don't listen, do you?' he said, putting one hand on a shoulder and giving it a quick squeeze.

'I know. First it was Jonathan giving me hell for coming in to see Pa and then Pa started in. Now you don't need to take it up. I had to come see how he is and I'm glad I did,' Cord said, sitting down again.

'I spoke to Little Jon as he was riding out,' Cookie said. 'He told me you were here. I hope he keeps his mouth shut in town.'

'Damn fool boy going into town?' the rancher asked. 'Guess my orders don't mean much. I tell him to stay on the ranch and he don't listen. Nobody listens to a sick man.'

'It ain't like that, Pa. I came in to see you and see how you are. There's still work to be done on the round-up and getting the drive started. I'll be gone long before daybreak. But I just can't sit out there waiting for some fool to come poking around.'

'Don't worry yourself about the gather or the drive to market. I talked with Casey Lewis. He's a good hand and the men will listen to him. Hell's fire, those boys know what has to be done and they'll do it. Don't let that worry you none.'

Cookie had been silent for a time, then he pushed away from the wall he'd been leaning against and said he'd be going to bed. 'Cord, stop off for a word when you leave, will you?'

After he left, Cord and his father talked a while, all the time the older man trying to convince his son that he was getting better. Later, as he'd said he would, Cord headed for the bunkhouse. With all the hands out on the round-up, the cook and Freddie were the only ones in the long room. He found both the men in their blankets, the young cook's helper snoring softly in his bunk.

'Boy, I just want to talk to you about things,' Cookie said. He sat up and rolled a cigarette. After setting a match to it, he carefully rubbed the fire out between his fingers. 'I got a funny feeling about something and I don't know exactly how to bring it up.'

'It's about Jonathan, isn't it?' Cord said, and watched as the cook's head nodded in agreement.

'I got thinking about that ribbon they say you left behind at the stage hold-up. About the only person who coulda picked it up was Jonathan. And he has been spending a lot of time in town, at that gambling-hall, I figure. I don't know, but I'd be willing to bet a month's pay the trouble all has to do with his gambling.'

'That's about the way I had it figured. He hasn't really been himself ever since his ma died. Leastways, he hasn't been acting like he should.'

'Your pa has always treated you two about the same; if anything he was easier on Jonathan. Well, it ain't none of my business, excepting it kind of is, you know?'

'Yeah. There's been times I wondered whether *you* were really my pa, the way you treated me. But you've always been around and willing to listen when I had a problem. Guess you can't help now. Jonathan is choosing his way and there isn't much anyone can do about that.'

'Well, you be damn careful, boy. You stay hid for a couple more days and I'll talk to Marshal Butterfield. I'll come out and find you once we get a few things straight-ened out.'

CHAPTER 27

Buck was able to stay out of sight for the rest of the day. The game of hide-and-seek really started when he watched, from a mile or so away, the miners come boiling out of the gully. For a while they milled around, trying to decide in which direction to go. Splitting up into smaller groups, they fanned out searching for some sign of Buck's passing. As he rode away he kept to the lowest ground, making his way farther back into the wild country. Some time later he came upon a small creek, where he watered the black horse and filled his canteen. Though he wished for a cup of coffee, he decided it wasn't safe yet.

For the rest of the afternoon he rode in what he hoped was the opposite direction to the posse, always heading, in a roundabout way, back toward the badlands. Once, hearing some gunfire way off in the distance, he worried about Cord. The young man had to know the lie of the land better than either Buck or the miners, but if he came upon them unaware it could be bad. There was nothing he could do about it, though, so he put the young Calhoun out of his mind.

It was after sundown when Buck eventually rode into the brush-choked gulch where he had camped. Sitting out of view in the last of the day's light, he took a long look over the country. Not seeing any movement, he turned and rode to the small spring.

With the horse secured nearby, he built up a small fire and quickly cooked a meal of bacon slices and hot coffee. He emptied a tin of sliced peaches to finish his supper, the first food he'd had all day. Sitting with his back to the rock wall, he relaxed with a smoke and thought about the next day. Somehow he was going to have to get around the miners and into town. The only way was to get the marshal on his side. Otherwise, sooner or later he'd get cornered and end up having to shoot some men he didn't want to hurt.

He pinched out his cigarette, checked to see that the horse had enough room to roll. Then he pulled his blanket up and fell asleep.

The moon was close to setting when Buck came awake. The big black horse had smelled or seen something and the loud exhalation of surprise brought the man out of a dreamless sleep. He rolled out of his blanket and crouched, his right hand already full of his Colt. Motionless, he waited for some indication what had caused the stallion to make the almost quiet snort. For a time there was nothing, not even the usual night sounds.

Looking up at the stars, Buck figured daylight was not far off. When he heard nothing out of the ordinary, he was just about to see if he could build up his fire when he heard the sound of a horse walking. Fading deeper in the darkness of the wall, he waited.

'Hey, Buck,' the voice called softly out of the darkness.

Relaxing, Buck stood up and answered. 'That had better be you, Cord. And you had better be bringing some good news.'

Leading his horse by the reins, the young man walked into the camp. He stripped the saddle and bridle from the animal, then hobbled it and turned to Buck.

'I could sure use a cup of hot coffee.'

'Well, just before you came barging in, I was thinking the same. Of course that pack of miners that chased me all over the place yesterday might like to come in for some too.'

'Naw. They're all rolled in their blankets over yonder, in the basin. That's where I was headed until I smelled the smoke of their camp-fire. Thought it was the miners so I came on around, hoping I'd find you here so I could warn you.'

Quickly, as he started the small fire and while setting up the pot of water next to it, Buck told him about his escape. Cord, sipping the hot liquid, told the big man all about his visit to the Rocking C.

'Whatever we do, I'd say we ought to be ready for another day of keeping out of that posse's sight,' Cord suggested. 'According to what the marshal told Pa, the father of that lady-friend of yours, old man Wilson, has been supplying food and bullets to the miners. I'd say that means they are out for blood, yours and mine.'

'So, what do you have to suggest?'

'I don't know. First I'd like to catch a few hours' sleep, though. Both me and my horse have been too long on the trail.'

Early the next morning, after brushing down their horses and saddling up, they made a quick fire, heated water for coffee and cooked the last of Buck's bacon. Rolling a cigarette afterwards, Buck looked over to the other man.

'I guess I don't understand why you're protecting

Jonathan. Didn't you tell me last night that you think he could be the only one who could get a hold of that ribbon?'

Cord looked down at the handful of sand he'd been picking up and let it flow out of his hand. He nodded. 'Yeah. From the day Pa brought Molly and him to the ranch, I've been taking care of him. That was what Pa told me to do.' Smiling, he glanced up at Buck. 'I've been doing it for so long I can't just stop.'

Buck was saved from having to respond when his horse blew. He rose to his feet, looked down toward the opening and, holding up one hand, listened. Hearing an outbreak of yelling and cursing, the two men swung into their saddles and turned toward the ridge. They crossed over and quickly dropped out of view of the campsite. Soon they were lost in one of a series of ravines that fanned out. With Cord leading at a brisk walk, the two horsemen were soon feeling safe again, at least for a while.

'Those men aren't about to give up, I'm thinking,' Buck said when they pulled up to take a breather. 'I doubt whether they could find us back in here, but then again I'm not sure I can find us either. Any ideas?'

'Yeah. Keep running until we can find a place to fight back.'

'What, and shoot them all? That isn't likely to happen.'

'OK. There's a falling-down cabin back over that series of ridges where we could hide out. Wait for darkness and then slip around and into town. There's water there and not many people know it. We use it as a campsite when hunting.'

The sun was high overhead when they rode out of the wide, sand-bottomed ravine and into the tall-wild-grass-covered meadow. Buck stopped in surprise. They had spent the morning riding up one gully and down another, Cord leading the way with confidence. Buck figured he could get out of the badlands if he had to, but he would admit if asked . . . he was lost.

The meadow wasn't very big, covering no more than a few acres. A small grove of pine-trees at the upper end indicated that water was there. Almost out of sight, a small log cabin, missing most of its roof, was half-hidden in the trees, giving proof that in the past some other use had been made of that piece of land. The cabin, Cord explained as they sat looking it over, had been used by the Calhouns whenever they were hunting in the country around the meadow. A nice, fresh-water spring bubbled out of the rocky hillside just to one side of the weather-beaten shack.

Difficult as it was to get through the gullies and ravines of this edge of the badlands to the meadow, only someone who had grown up in that area and had hunted it would have known the best trail to take to get there.

After they had watered the horses and put them on leads, Cord started a fire in the smoke-blackened rock-lined fire-pit in front of the cabin, and started heating water. Buck, after exploring around a little, settled down on his heels and rolled a smoke.

'That the only way in here?' he asked, pointing down toward the bottom of the meadow, the way they had come in.

'No. Back there, behind the trees, is a steep trail up onto the ridge. From there it drops down into the head of that basin. The creek that feeds that little valley is just on the other side of that wall behind here.'

'So, would that be the quickest way out of here, and toward town?'

'Yeah. The climb looks a lot worse than it is. The horses can make it pretty easy.'

The posse of miners came into the meadow just as the morning sun was peeking over the far ridge. This time they rode quietly out of the same gully Cord and Buck had come along the day before. Buck, having just put the sand-scoured fry-pan into a saddle-bag, looked up and saw them filing into the high grass.

'Cord,' he said quietly. He pointed down at the men a few hundred yards away, took the black's reins and followed Cord around the cabin and into the trees before climbing into the saddle. As quickly and quietly as they could, the two horses wound around the trees, following the faint trail. Out of sight of the men below, they reached the last of the trees and found themselves on a slender trail. Looking back, Buck could see that for a stretch they would be in plain sight of the miners.

Before they could move on, they turned to watch as one of the men below yelled. Sitting their saddles, they saw the riders, at the signal, jab their ponies in the side and, yelling as loudly as they could, charge the cabin. As quickly as the charge began, it ended, with not a shot fired. Now, if they knew what to look for, they would be coming around the shack.

'Better get on up the trail, Cord, while they're trying to figure out where we are.' Close behind him, Buck kept one eye on the trail ahead while glancing back. Gunfire brought him to a halt as he turned back. Below, standing out from the cabin, two of the miners were aiming their rifles up at the horsemen.

Shooting uphill was a chancy thing at best, Buck knew, but it wouldn't take but a little luck to score a hit. He pulled his rifle from its holster, quickly levered a shell and, without taking much aim, fired.

Cord, a little farther up the trail, had done the same and as the men below found themselves out in the open, they ducked back into the trees.

The two men turned and continued up the trail, trying to get far enough ahead to be safe when the posse found the bottom of the trail. Shooting down was a little better than shooting up and Buck believed he could keep anyone from hurrying up after them.

At one point in the long climb up out of the little valley, the trail curled around a huge outcropping of weathered sandstone. Cord had disappeared around it and Buck was just up to it when a bullet struck the rock inches from his head. The loud booming told him that one of the miners was armed with a Sharps .50.

Anyone knowing how to shoot one of the long-barreled weapons would be able to hit a spot a mile away. That brought most of the trail into the Sharps's range. Urging the black forward, Buck saw that the outcropping wasn't big enough for both riders.

CHAPTER 28

The sun's heat against the wall would become a worry as the day wore on, even if there were enough room behind the outcropping to cover both horses and their riders. The men had filled their canteens, but that wouldn't be enough for long. The horses, jammed together as they were, would soon cause trouble, too.

The rifleman with the long rifle had settled down and started hitting too close to anything hanging out. If a piece of flying rock hit one of the horses, that'd be it. Buck, careful not to expose himself, looked down. There the man was, standing just out of the trees with his rifle supported on a forked stick. Even as he watched, the man pulled the trigger, the heavy slug hitting the rock-face inches above Buck's head. He ducked back, almost spooking Cord's horse. The noise and sudden movements were making the piebald nervous.

'Well, partner,' said Buck, 'the only thing I see to do is, when that jasper fires the next time, for you to take off up the trail. That Sharps is a single-shot and it takes a minute or so for him to reload and then get his aim. If you're moving, he won't be able to get settled so there isn't much chance he could hit anything. At the same time I'll start shooting back. That'll make him nervous.'

'And then what? I'll be up there and you'll still be down here, trapped behind this rock. Those other fellows won't be sitting still, either, they'll be ready for something like that.'

Once again, the big rifle sent a slug into the edge of the covering rock, causing the piebald to jerk at the tightly held reins.

'Yeah,' Buck agreed, 'but that's the only answer I've got. When you get up there a bit, maybe there's another hidey-hole you can duck into and give me some cover. We certainly can't stay here.'

'OK, you win. When he fires again, I'm off.'

The wait wasn't long and the next shot came when Cord, getting ready, got too close to the upper edge of the rock. The instant he heard the roar of the Sharps, he was moving. His horse, needing no urging, nearly ran over him.

Buck, levering his rifle as fast as he could, fired shot after shot at the rifleman, forcing him back to safety. As he reloaded, he looked down and saw that a few braver souls had started up the trail. Quickly shooting almost straight down, he sent them hurrying back into the cover of the trees. For a few minutes it was quiet.

'Hey, Buck,' Cord called down, 'come on up. There's good cover here and I've got a clear shot both at that fellow with the big rifle and anyone coming up the trail.' His voice was loud enough to carry down to the attackers. Smiling and with his rifle ready in one hand, Buck pulled the black horse from behind the rock and up the trail.

Cord was ready and when someone below moved to shoot up at the moving man, he chased him back to cover with a well-placed shot. As he caught up to Cord, Buck saw that the trail left the climb at that point and disappeared in a forest of tall trees.

'Come on,' Cord yelled, already in the saddle and heading out.

Laughing with relief, Buck quickly followed.

Having decided that they could do without coffee or a hot meal, the two men found a place along the creek in the basin that gave them the cover they needed. They hobbled their horses close by and took turns sitting up, wrapped in a blanket, listening for trouble. Neither man got much sleep and by the first sign of daybreak, they were riding south.

Buck was again heading for a talk with the marshal and Cord dropped off to stop by the ranch. Someone was going to have to find a way out of this mess; they agreed that getting chased all over the country wasn't an answer.

CHAPTER 29

Once more, after quietly unsaddling his tired horse in the big barn and rubbing him down with handfuls of straw, Cord waited in the darkness of the barn door. He had timed his visit so as to get to the back of the barn just as darkness fell, and now, after making sure none of the hands was enjoying a last smoke before turning in, he made his way from shadow to shadow across the front porch. Silently he opened the front door and slipped in, as quietly closing the door behind him.

Again waiting and listening, he stood by the front wall.

'Well, if you're gonna come in, come in,' a soft voice from across the room broke the silence. Cookie. Cord relaxed, thinking he shouldn't have expected to catch the old man sleeping. 'As for being a sneaky Indian, boy,' the soft voice continued with a laugh behind the words, 'you got a lot to learn. I heard you splashing across the creek behind the barn. C'mon, your pa is waiting for you. Don't get all panicky, but there is someone wants to talk to you.'

Still shaking a bit from being surprised, Cord walked past the ranch cook and headed down to his pa's bedroom. Upon opening that door he first saw his pa still flat on his back, then saw what Cookie was talking about. Sitting in the chair by the bedside was Marshal Butterfield.

'Hey, son. Good of you to stop by,' his pa said, weakness showing in his voice. 'Old mister lawman thought you might be coming by sooner or later. He's been waiting for darkness, just as you did, I figure.'

'Hiyah, Cord.' The tall man stood to reach across the bed to shake hands. 'I was hoping you'd come in tonight. I'd have sent someone out looking for you if you hadn't.'

Cookie, leaning against a wall, nodded. 'Well, Cord. What do you have to say for yourself? I thought you were going to stay hidden out for a while.'

'Staying hidden is getting harder all the time. There's been so much traffic through that end of the ranch that I kept expecting a wagonload of church folks taking a picnic at any time. Too bad, 'cause that has always been darned good country to stay out of sight in. Least it was.'

A weak laugh broke the silence. 'Boy, from what I'm hearing, you fellows really kicked the can over. Broke one fella's shoulder and put another on crutches. I guess it was a good thing that somewhere along the way you learned to shoot straight. Leastways you didn't kill any of those idiots.'

'That was Buck's doing. He almost got trapped back in the badlands. I figure he could've left a few more lying there if he'd wanted to. I wasn't there but, thinking about it, I have to admit I might have taken better aim and dropped anyone if I'd had a good shot at anyone other than the miners. Neither Buck nor I have any quarrel with those folks; they think they're doing the right thing. But they've been getting some help from someone, and I don't like that.' Cord was trying to watch the faces of both his pa and the marshal at the same time. 'That crowd knew how to get up into the meadow and they really expected to trap us there. Marshal, how do you figure that gang knew where we were?'

Try as he might, Cord could read nothing in any of the men's faces. Gawd, he said to himself, I'd hate to play high-stakes poker with this group.

Without changing his blank expression, Marshal Butterfield passed over the question. 'Those miners are getting tired of hanging around. I figure that sooner or later the jokers will get tired of chasing shadows and let's hope they'll go back up north. That's when I can do my job without having some idiot with pounds of muck and grit under his fingernails following my every move. So far it hasn't worked out that way.'

'What happened?' Cord asked. 'I didn't recognize any of the men in that gang, I accepted that they were just the bunch of miners after us.'

'Maybe a few of them were miners but there were also a lot of cowboys who are out of work. John, your drive to the railhead is among the last for this region this fall. That means there's a lot of drovers that'll be looking for anything to tide them through the winter. No, I hate to say it, but about half of those men riding with the miners were men who'll be riding the grub-line in the near future.'

'Who's paying them?' Cookie asked, quietly. 'The miners have a stake in finding that payroll, but someone's got to be feeding and taking care of any other help.'

'Yep,' the marshal said, nodding in agreement. 'Those boys'll want to be paid for everything from feed for their horses to their own grub, not to mention any lead and powder they burn. That's where it gets interesting. I expect that that gambler, Henley, is putting up a few dollars, but I could probably never prove it. No, the surprising thing is where the food and ammunition is coming from.'

Butterfield stopped and looked first at the bedridden

rancher, then directly at Cord. 'I've got it on good authority that most of that stuff is from the back door of Wilson's store.'

Cord was speechless. John Calhoun waited a bit, then asked, 'Why would he do that? He certainly didn't lose anything in the stage hold-up, so why would he help finance any posse?'

Shaking his head, Cord said, 'He couldn't hate me that much, could he?'

'Well, I don't know,' Butterfield said. 'I do know he's been awfully protective of that daughter of his. Seems your friend Buck got too close to her at the dance a while back and he's been anxious about getting rid of what he sees as a threat. Another member of the posse that came back into town was a guy named Stokes. He's awfully close to Henley and sits in on the poker games in the Star. The same ones that your step-brother has been sitting in on. You ask how Henley and his crew knew where you were hiding and I can't tell you. But it does look suspicious, don't it?'

'No,' came the strong, hard voice from his bed. 'I just won't believe Jonathan would help set up something like that. He might be acting somewhat questionable, I'll grant, but throw his brother to the dogs? No, he wouldn't do that.'

Nobody responded to his outburst. Eventually, shaking his head, Butterfield looked up. 'Well, son, what now? You can't go back to hiding and I certainly ain't making any headway with the hold-up. The miners are starting to give it up, but there's folks in town who are wanting to take up the chase. There ain't much I can do; the question is, what're you two gonna do?'

'I don't know what to do,' Cord said in frustration.

'Buck has gone on into town to talk with you. He says the fossil-hunters, Cole and his people, can prove he was where he was when that stage was robbed. What do you think we should do, Pa?'

'Dammit it, boy, having the law on our side helps, but not if you're caught. Turning yourself in might help, but as far as I can see, the sign is against you. I don't know what you can do, but you gotta do something, that's clear.'

'Well,' Cord said, looking his pa in the eye, 'one thing I can maybe do is clear up the question of how Jonathan is involved. A little talk with him won't hurt none, I reckon.'

CHAPTER 30

Cord didn't take any chances. He had discussed his plans, such as they were, with the marshal. Those plans were to simply ride in toward town and try to catch Jonathan as he was coming back to the ranch.

According to the cook, since John had taken to his bed, Jonathan had been spending almost every night in town, returning at just about daybreak in time to turn out with the rest of the crew. Cord figured that if he could talk with his step-brother without anyone on hand to give advice or influence, he might find out what was going on. If that didn't work, well, Cord would just have to come up with something else, or hope that Buck did.

Cord took up a spot just outside of town, near the fork in the main road, tied his horse to a tree-branch and settled down to wait. This was a favorite time of day for the young man. The cool night air was still, and the only noise was from the seldom heard creatures of the night. With his back to the tree, he looked over the moonlit opening in the trees that was the road as an owl silently passed low over the grass. Thinking about the situation he was in, his thoughts came around to Julie and her father.

It was true he'd only talked to the girl a few times and then danced with her. A city girl. In his growing-up years, there had been little contact with girls of his own age. About the only females he had seen had been ranchers' wives, and he only met those when in town picking up supplies. Talking with Julie had been easy, though. Almost too easy, as if they had been friends for years. Thinking about dancing with her caused his face to heat up. Holding her and swinging her around the dance floor had been like, well, he thought, like floating.

A faint squealing noise brought his attention back to the job at hand. The owl, he figured, had been successful in his hunt. Shortly after, he heard the quiet clopping of a walking horse on the road. He moved silently to the side of the track and watched as a rider, head bowed as if asleep, came his way slowly. When the rider left the shadow of the trees and rode into the moonlight, Cord could see it was Jonathan.

The horse must have seen Cord standing by the side of the road and didn't snort or act startled. Stopping next to the standing man, he nuzzled Cord's hand as if searching for a treat. Jonathan, with a mumbled curse, jabbed his mount in the side, but Cord was holding the headstall and the horse didn't move. That brought the rider's head up.

'What the hell—' he said questioning, then, recognizing Cord in the moonlight, he came wide awake. 'What are you doing?'

'I figure you and I should have a little talk, brother.'

'There ain't nothing I've got to talk to you about. Hell, half the country is out looking for you and that drifter friend of yours, wanting to hang the bad stagecoach robbers. You'd be better getting out of the country, than stopping innocent people on their way home.'

'Now that is one of the things I want to talk to you about. Come on over here and let's set and see what we can find out.' Still holding the headgear, Cord turned and walked back into the shadows. The horse followed, even with Jonathan sawing at the reins.

'I have nothing to talk to you about and I ain't gonna sit down with you.'

Cord didn't respond, simply jerked the reins from Jonathan's hands and tied them to a tree branch. Not even looking up at the mounted man, Cord suddenly grabbed Jonathan's leg and lifted, tossing the rider out of the saddle. Hurrying around the horse before the smaller man could get to his feet, he took a handful of shirt and pulled, forcing him into a sitting position.

'Now,' Cord said quietly, 'I reckon you can sit down with your brother after all.'

Wiping a sleeve across his face, Jonathan snorted. 'I ain't your brother. And I ain't got nothing to say to you.'

'Let's see what you can come up with. How about the question of how your gambling friend found us up at the hunting cabin in the badlands? Or how did that blue ribbon end up at the stagecoach hold-up. I'm sure you've got some answers to those questions.'

'Naw. I don't know what you're talking about,' Jonathan answered, and then, looking up, smiled. 'But I will tell you this. That brown-haired girlfriend that clerks in her pa's store? I been talking with her. She don't know that big cowboy real good and was asking what kind of man he is. Boy, did I tell her. Don't be surprised if she doesn't want anything to do with him ever again. And her pa? Ha. Guess you know how he feels about cowboys. A no-good thieving cowboy, is what his idea of old Buck Armstrong is. Yah, I done my talking to those folks.'

'Why you. . . .' Cord said, clenching a fist and rearing back, before stopping.

'Yeah, big brother,' said Jonathan sneeringly, 'even if you get yourself out of the hold-up, your chances with that fossil-hunter's daughter, or Mr Big Shot Armstrong's with Miss Priss the Widow are dead. The chances are good though, that that's how you're both gonna find yourselves. Dead. Luther Henley don't like it when someone gets in his way, and that's gonna be the end of you both. No girl and a gang of shooters dogging your every move. Now, brother, anything else you want to talk about?'

CHAPTER 31

Still unable to deal with his step-brother as he wanted, Cord could only watch as the younger man got on his horse and headed back toward town, his laughter echoing in the early morning's stillness long after the sound of his horse faded away.

Leaning against a tree trunk, Cord let his head droop. As Jonathan had so joyously pointed out, half the country was looking for him and Buck. Cord didn't say it, but his chance of getting to know the Cole girl wasn't too good, not while everyone thought he was a stagecoach robber. Nowhere could he see that he had any future at all. It looked like the only way out for him was to get out of this part of Utah. Maybe he could start over in California or somewhere in the Oregon Territory. He'd have to talk to Buck. He'd know.

Daylight found Buck riding slowly and quietly out of the brush behind Elizabeth's little house. Leaving the big black horse tied to a tree limb, he pulled his hat down low to cover his face and he sauntered around to the front of her house. Quietly he knocked on her door.

'Buck! What are you doing here? Don't you know half the men in town are looking for you and Cord? Come in, quick!' Opening the door wide she looked up and down the street as the big man passed by her.

'To tell the truth, I'm in town to talk with the marshal and, of course, to see you. If Cord can go riding out to court Julie Cole while all those miners are beating the brush for him, then I guess I can come in here to see you, can't I?' He smiled.

'You men,' she said exasperatedly. She took a mug from a shelf and poured him a cup of coffee. He settled into a kitchen chair, dropped his hat on the floor and blew the steam from the hot coffee.

'Of course I'm happy you did come to see me,' she went on, still sounding a bit flustered and scared, 'but it isn't just the miners who are looking for the two of you. A lot of out-of-work cowhands have joined in. It's almost as if someone has put up a ransom for your capture. Buck . . .' she hesitated, 'you didn't have anything to do with that hold-up, did you?' Before he could answer, she shook her head. 'No, why am I even asking? Of course you didn't. Cord's brother has been talking and naturally, any talk against any cowboy my father hears becomes gospel as far as he's concerned.'

'No, I'm afraid neither of us had anything to do with it. And take anything that young Calhoun says with a big grain of salt. He's not really Cord's brother and the two haven't been getting along for quite some time, I'm told. Your father? One of these days you're going to fall for somebody and it won't matter whether he likes it or not.'

'Maybe I already have, Buck. Have you thought of that?'

He took a quick look up from his coffee and frowned. 'Maybe I'd better not get too comfortable, not until I get a few things cleared up.' He picked his hat up, rose to his feet, and quickly thanked the woman for the coffee. Then, first looking around before stepping out, he left her standing in the doorway.

Trying to recall exactly where the marshal's office was, he walked down the back street, trying not to be seen in the early-morning light. Not seeing any signs or any indication of where the lawman would be, he slipped between two buildings and looked up and down the town's main street. Not seeing anyone, he stepped out far enough to see where he was. He spotted the sign hanging out over the boardwalk and turned in that direction. Stepping as lightly as he could, Buck quietly opened the office door.

'Well, young man, I've been expecting you.' A man's voice from the dark room brought him to a halt, outlined in the open door.

Marshal Butterfield struck a wooden match and lit the wick of the lantern sitting on his desk. 'Well, don't just stand there waiting until one of damn fools sees you, come on in.'

Buck let his half-drawn revolver drop back into his holster and closed the door. 'Marshal, you just scared the geewillikers out of me. Let's just wait until my heart gets to beating again.' He took the chair the lawman waved him to and sat down. 'You sound as if you expected me?'

'Yep, I figured you'd get here sooner or later. After talking with Cord out at the Rocking C, it seemed likely.'

'You talked with Cord, huh? Tell me, how do you know I didn't have a hand in stopping that payroll stage?'

'Nope. If Cord wasn't part of it, and he said you weren't, that's good enough for me. 'Course, there isn't that many people in town that'd think that way. Especially with everybody like that dumb storekeeper and the gambler talking the way they have been. I don't know if you heard, but Cord's little brother has been spreading the word against

Cord and you, too.'

'Yeah, Elizabeth mentioned it. I haven't got that all figured out yet.'

'Cord said he was going to have a talk with Jonathan, but I think it's a case of Luther Henley getting his hooks into the boy. Old John mentioned some time ago that the boy had gotten himself into debt over a poker game. It just doesn't seem likely that he'd go so far as to turn away from John and Cord, though.'

'So what do I do, Marshal? The Coles can tell you about where I was when the stage was held up and Cord can prove he was out working the gather, but how do we get that gang of miners off our backs?'

'I haven't figured that out yet. The best thing we can do right now, though, is to get you back outa here. The Rocking C is probably the best place to talk about what's next. Where'd you leave your horse?'

Not caring who saw him, Cord rode back to the ranch after leaving Jonathan, as if he didn't have a care in the world, coming from the road right up to the big house just as the sun cleared the far hills. Still early in the morning, the work crew had already left for the holding-ground, leaving the ranch looking quiet and empty. He tied off to the porch railing and walked over to the cook shack just as the ranch cook came out through the door.

'Hey, boy. What are you thinking, riding right up like nobody's hunting you?'

'Cookie, I don't really care. I just had a long talk with Jonathan. He's been working with Henley all along. To top it off, he's been talking against me and Buck to Elizabeth's father, so old man Wilson's drumming up support for the miners. As far as I can see, there ain't much I can do except leave this part of the country.'

'No, Cord. Take my word for it, running won't solve anything. C'mon, let's talk to your dad about this. He won't like hearing about Jonathan, but it's time he took off the blinders.'

'Ah, hell, Cookie. I haven't had a good feed in quite a while. My stomach is growling so loud I can't sleep. Let's go see what you can rustle up for me before talking to Pa.'

As usual, the big smoke-blackened coffeepot was on the back of the cook-stove and even before Cord had taken a seat at the big table that the crew used Freddie had a cup poured.

'I 'spect you're on the hungry side.' The cook's helper laughed. 'Traipsing all around the country, you probably missed a few meals, I reckon.' Chuckling, he lifted the lid on the firebox and stoked up the stove.

'Don't go be spending all day laughing, boy. Get the man a plate and some tools.' The ranch cook smiled at Cord. 'I suppose he's right, though. And of course you can just barge in any time of the day but never think about stopping off for some grub to take along. Well, I'll tell you, this is your lucky day. I just happen to have a few eggs and some rotten old bacon handy.'

Cord watched as the old man scraped off the top of the huge cook-stove with a spatula before breaking half a dozen eggs onto the heated surface. At the cook's direction, Freddie sliced bread that was put to brown on one side of the hot stove, next to a few thick rashers of bacon. Sipping the hot, black coffee, Cord watched as his breakfast was prepared.

Taking his time after finishing the meal, Cord sat back in the chair and relaxed with a second cup of the strong brew. Leaving the ranch where he had grown up would be tough, he thought. No more listening to the old grouchy cook, and no more workingman's breakfasts. All the plans that he and his pa had discussed for the ranch would have to be forgotten. The plans he had just begun thinking about, bringing a bride out to make the place a real home, raising a new family and teaching his own sons about ranching and hunting and all the things that he'd been taught, these would all have to be forgotten. He didn't know how much it would bother Buck to ride away from all this trouble, but it likely wouldn't be easy for him either.

Nodding his thanks to Cookie and his helper, Cord left the cook shack and headed slowly for the big house. As he came through the back door he stopped at hearing loud voices coming from his pa's bedroom. He pushed through that door and was brought to a halt at the sight of Jonathan standing in the corner across from Pa's bed. The smile on his face was more of a smirk as he watched the look on Cord's face.

CHAPTER 32

'Looks like we got here just in time, Mr Henley. Here's the man of the hour, just finished with a hearty breakfast,' Jonathan said through the smirking grin as the door behind Cord was slammed shut. Cord turned his head and saw that the gambler had been standing out of sight. Standing a few feet away and facing Henley were Buck and the marshal.

'Pa,' Cord asked the shrunken man in the bed, 'you all right?'

'Naw, I ain't all right. What's this all about, Cord? Old Butterfield and Armstrong was just starting to tell me some tall tales about Little Jon here, when first those two came busting in and then you come crashing in. What the hell's going on, boy?'

'Now that's what we're here to straighten out, old man,' Jonathan said, calmly pulling a six-gun and holding it pointed in Cord's direction. 'And I ain't "Little" anything. Not no more.' Catching the look on Cord's face, he swung the gun up. 'No, don't go thinking you can pull your iron before I can jerk this trigger. Ha. Look at you. Thinking you're the only one who can sneak across the creek and get into the house unseen. And all the time you're having your last meal. Hey, Mr Henley, the condemned man ate a

154

hearty last meal,' he said laughing at his own joke.

Slowly pulling the makings from a shirt pocket, Buck looked across at the young man and calmly started rolling a cigarette. 'What're you planning on doing, boy? We figured out how the blue ribbon got left at the hold-up, and how you made sure your gambling partner here heard all about where Cord and I would likely go for a hideout, but what's the point of coming in here now?'

Looking back at Henley as he mentioned him, Buck saw how the man was standing. Not leaning against the wall, but relaxed with his hands loosely holding the lapels of his coat, a small smile on his narrow face. A smile that, Buck noted, didn't reach his hard, cold eyes.

'C'mon, boy.' Henley's hard, dry voice prodded Jonathan. 'Let's get on with it.'

'Now, what would that be, boy,' Buck asked, stressing the last word, as he struck a wooden match with one thumbnail and put fire to his quirly. 'What does this bucko have planned for you? Another stage robbery? More horse-rustling? You were part of that, weren't you?'

'Yes, damn it. If you hadn't butted in none of this would have happened. There'd be enough money from those nags to pay off what I owe Mr Henley. But no, there you come, being the big hero. Well, now there's no reason for any more of that.' Jonathan laughed. 'Nope. Think about it. Here's the men everyone is looking for, the great high-waymen themselves, right here in front of my gun.'

'What are your plans for me, boy,' Butterfield asked, also stressing the last word.

'Ha. That's easy. How was it that these two learned about the payroll? How come they seem to know about all the miners and bums that're out trying to catch them? The answer is easy. You, Mr High and Mighty lawman, you just had to get in the way. I suppose people will believe me when I tell them you were actually part of that hold-up gang. Nobody'll miss you.'

'C'mon, Jonathan. That's enough talking, get on with it,' Henley demanded. Buck watched as the gambler's right hand seemed to move a bit from the coat lapel. Glancing at Cord, he saw that under the quiet relaxed stance, he was really tense and ready. Buck decided he'd watch Henley's right hand.

'Naw, Mr Henley. Let me tell them what we got planned. It should be clear, anyhow. With you dead,' he tipped the barrel of his pistol at Cord, 'that leaves me the only heir this old man's got, now don't it? So there ain't no need to run any more little jags of horse flesh to the rail-head. It'll all be mine.' Now the pistol was aimed square on Cord's chest.

'How you gonna get rid of me?' John Calhoun's weak question came from the blanket-covered bed. 'You think I'll just go along with this dumb idea?'

'Nope. A pillow over your head and everybody'll think you died a natural death.'

Buck glanced slowly down at his cigarette and asked in his quiet voice, 'And what then, boy? This friend of yours sets you up to help steal a few head and then got you involved with that stage hold-up. Now he's gonna have the ranch. Do you really think he'll sit by after all this and let you play the big man? No, I don't reckon you'll be in the driver's seat for long. By the way, did you ever get your share of that payroll? Where is it?'

'Mr Henley's ideas have paid off so far, and so will this one. The payroll? It's safe, hear me, it's safe.' Jonathan's laugh sounded thin in the closed room.

Buck, now watching Henley's hands, wasn't watching

Cord but at the sound of a gun going off somewhere behind him he was ready for the gambler's reaction. As the silver pistol came out of the hidden shoulder holster, Buck had already jerked his .44 up and was firing. Henley, thrown back as the big slug took him in the chest, crumpled. Before the dead man's body hit the floor, Buck was swinging around to face Jonathan only to stop as he saw the younger man leaning tiredly against the wall, his gun hand empty and hanging at his side.

'You . . .' he said weakly as he slid down to end up sitting with his back to the wall and his legs outstretched, 'you shot me.'

Expecting to see Cord holding his handgun, Buck was surprised to see that both the young man's hands were empty.

'Oh, Gawd.' Big John's weak voice was trembling. 'I had to shoot him. Oh, Gawd.' Leaning over the bed, Buck saw the old man's octagonal-barreled pistol lying on the blanket at the sick man's side. Slowly the old man's eyes closed and for the first time since falling off the horse, the pain was gone from his face.

CHAPTER 33

'We buried Pa up on the ridge,' Cord was telling Marshal Butterfield the next day, 'up in next to where we'd put Molly so long ago. Jonathan is buried on the other side of her grave. I didn't want him there, but Buck and Cookie talked me into it. Guess Pa would have liked it that way. He never did believe Little Jon was a bad one.'

Having brought Henley's body into town in the back of a wagon, Cord and the big cowboy had stopped at the Marshal's office. After telling their story, the three men, with a growing crowd following, walked across to the saloon. With very little prompting from the law, Henry pointed out the saloon-owner's safe. Butterfield took out the key he had found in the dead gambler's pocket and unlocked the big, black steel safe. There, along with a sack filled with wallets and a few pieces of jewelry, still wrapped in paper bands, was the mine payroll. All at once, the crowd was silent.

'Well, I guess that takes care of who really robbed the payroll stage, doesn't it, boys?' Marshal Butterfield asked, his words hard and demanding. Slowly, one at a time at first and then in a small rush, the remaining miners left the building.

Butterfield, looking over at Cord, smiled. 'I'd say the

only thing left for you to do is go get a new piece of ribbon for your hat.'

'I don't know, Marshal,' Buck said quietly as he leaned against the bar. Motioning to Henry to pour a whiskey for the three of them, he slowly shook his head. 'As I recall, that young girl's pa don't take to cowboys hanging around. Even if that fossil-hunter's daughter did seem to take a fancy to that ribbon, it might get a bit dangerous for the boy to go shopping over there.'

'Naw,' the marshal said, picking up the glass of dark liquor that the bartender had set in front of him, 'that little runt of a store owner likes money. He wouldn't dare get the owner of one of the biggest ranches around mad at him, now would he? What do you think, Cord?'

Leaving his whiskey on the bar, untouched, Cord Calhoun was already out through the swinging doors when the question was asked.

Elizabeth laughed as she told Buck how much in a hurry young Calhoun had been to buy the ribbon. 'Why, I'll bet he runs that poor pony of his into the ground, getting out to the Coles' camp. He said something about inviting her to the dance next Saturday night.' Looking down at her hands resting on the porch railing, she hesitated. 'Buck, will you be going to the dance?'

'Now, as I recall, the last dance involved a quiet walk home. I don't think I can afford to hang around for something like that again.' He stopped and then, when the woman started to speak, he shook his head. 'No, Elizabeth. It wouldn't do any good for me to stay here in Jensen any longer. You'll find yourself a good man, and that isn't me.'

He picked up the reins of his black stud horse and

smiled. 'Why, there I'd be getting all housebroke when the good Professor Fish sent me another letter asking for a favor. You'd just get your heart broken again.'

He swung into the saddler and looked down at her. Then, reaching his left hand up, he tipped his hat to her. As he rode down the back street he turned and waved. Then he headed toward the bridge and the road out of town.